# A Slice of Summer

# A Slice of Summer

## A Silver Falls Romance

## Melissa McClone

TULE
PUBLISHING

# Dedication

For the readers who wanted more Silver Falls.

Special thanks to Jennifer Niles for answering a million questions for me and the members of the Author Arena Writing club on Clubhouse. I wouldn't have finished this book without you.

# Chapter One

THE SILVER FALLS Summer Fair was less than a week away, but Taryn Lawson wasn't worried. It was only Monday, and the festival didn't start until Friday afternoon. She stepped out of her back door and onto the covered patio. Unlike the other First Avenue Business Association members, who'd spent last night's meeting in a panic over their booths not being finished yet, she had everything under control.

Pride surged through her, adding a bounce to her step. "This is my year."

She'd worked hard in the fall storing parts of the booth in the backyard shed before the weather changed. Now that the bakery's new patio seating area was open, she would prepare for the upcoming festival. It shouldn't take long. All she needed to do was remove the pieces, assemble them, transport them to the park, and add the final details.

Easy-peasy.

Warmth spread through her. Her parents wouldn't be able to complain about this.

As Taryn crossed the backyard, her tennis shoes sank into the tall grass. She'd neglected the lawn and hadn't mowed for far too long. The flower beds could use weeding, and the shrubs required trimming. Or was that pruning?

No matter.

Nothing would bring her down today.

She would take care of the yard soon. So what if she'd been saying those exact words ever since her parents retired and she took over running the place?

They were true. Eventually, she would have the time once she didn't feel as if the bakery and her future could be ripped away at any moment.

Sweat beaded at her neck. "It's going to be a scorcher today."

Not unusual for July, but she hoped the temperature wouldn't rise until closer to lunchtime. Still, a dose of vitamin D would do her good. The clear, blue sky meant more customers might visit the bakery's patio for dessert tonight. She shouldn't complain.

Taryn floated toward the shed, buoyed by an overflow of hope. If things went according to plan, business would return to normal by August. She rubbed her hands together.

She removed the padlock and opened the door.

Mildew assaulted her nose. "Ew."

She glanced inside. A smelly mess of wood, plastic, mold, and rot greeted her.

Taryn groaned. "No. This is not happening."

Her muscles bunched. Her eyes wanted to close, but she kept them open. Nothing would erase the disaster in front of her, including pretending.

*Out of sight, out of mind* wouldn't help.

She surveyed the items, her stomach dropping lower with each passing second. All her hard work on the *Midsummer Night's Dream*-themed booth was...

"It's all ruined."

Boulders settled in the pit of her stomach. The smell of rotted wood assaulted her nose.

So much for the framing she'd planned on using as the base for the decorations.

The pop-up tent canopy hadn't survived, either. Mold grew on the vinyl. Same for the signs she'd drawn.

Her shoulders sagged. "Ruined."

No wonder the used shed had been dirt cheap. The roof or seams—perhaps both—must leak. The previous owner had told her it worked fine and that it kept their lawn mower and yard tools dry and in excellent condition, so she'd never considered testing it.

Why would someone lie?

*To make the sale.*

But that had never crossed her mind.

Too trusting.

Taryn had heard it a million times. Her chest tightened. Guess people were right. She blew out a long breath.

Lesson learned. Even with the snow that fell this past winter, she would have been better off putting the pieces on her patio and covering them with tarps.

A trip to the dump would take care of the mess, but she'd planned on spending the morning preparing for her big build. Now, she would have to start over with only days to redo everything. At least she wouldn't be starting from scratch. Her plans were hanging on the bulletin board in the bakery's office.

"Might as well go to work." The resignation in her words matched her sagging shoulders. She trudged inside.

After slathering sunscreen on her arms and face, she set off for First Avenue with its quaint boutiques, cafés, and stores lining both sides of the street.

The rising temperature didn't stop the birds from singing in the tall maples nearby. The songs became nothing but white noise. With her mind on the booth, Taryn couldn't enjoy the sweet melodies.

*What am I going to do?*

Yes, the new patio and dessert menu appeared to be a hit with customers, but the upcoming fair was the second part of her plan to turn business around and what kept her from making hard decisions—ones she didn't want to make— about staffing needs now.

*Don't panic.*

*You have plenty of time.*

Knowing that didn't stop the churning in her stomach.

More than once, her father had mumbled about selling to the Summit Ridge Bakery owners since they knew what they were doing.

Unlike her had been implied.

The churning turned into a full-blown spin cycle.

It hurt knowing her dad felt that way when Taryn was doing the best she could and putting her all into the bakery. A part of her blamed Nick Baxter, a friend since high school involved with the new place. He used to come into Lawson's all the time, but he and Robin, his wife, hadn't been in since the other one opened.

Rumor suggested he hadn't been a standup guy when he sold his company out from under his co-founder and fellow classmate, Brandt Winslow, but Taryn had given both friends the benefit of the doubt. Now, Nick wanted to drive her out of business. Maybe she should have sided with Brandt.

But it wasn't only the Summit Ridge Bakery causing her grief. Her dad had voiced doubts about her abilities for years. But if he or Nick thought she would give up without fighting for what was hers, they were badly mistaken.

Taryn opened the bakery's front door, and an electronic ping sounded. The scent of fresh bread greeted her like an old friend. And it was. This place was her second home.

She'd grown up within these walls—learning to bake saying her ABCs; measuring ingredients provided her first lesson in fractions; and using the differences between liquid and dry items to understand volume. Baking was in her DNA. She'd never considered, never wanted, another job other than to run the bakery.

The bell dinged again when the door shut.

The second sound reminded staff to come to the counter if no one was out front. It worked better than the jingling of the old bell. Though replacing it led to a meltdown by her father.

A typical reaction.

Ever since Taryn took over running the bakery, her parents questioned each decision, big or small, she made, threatening not to sign the bakery over to her. She'd run every aspect of the business for three years, longer if she counted the years before her father retired, but he kept saying her handling the bakery alone was a trial run.

*Trial run!*

What else did she need to do to prove herself?

Jayden, her assistant manager, refilled the display case with baked goods. "Good morning."

He was the definition of tall at six feet two, dark with umber skin, and movie-star handsome with features that made customers take second and third looks. He was also a great baker. She counted him and Rachelle, his wife of ten years, among her closest friends.

He glanced up. "What happened?"

Taryn didn't know how he could read her so well. "What do you mean?"

"You're not smiling." His gaze narrowed. "And two little lines above the bridge of your nose show up when you're unhappy or upset."

"I…" She touched the spot between her eyebrows. "There are lines."

"Tell me what's going on."

Taryn blew out a breath. "Remember how I stored the summer fair booth in the storage shed I bought last September?"

"The used one you found in an ad online?"

She nodded. "Turns out it leaks. Moisture has ruined everything inside. The pieces are warped or covered in mold or both. I have to start from scratch."

Jayden glanced at the calendar—a fundraiser for the local fire department—hanging on the wall. "Isn't that—"

"This coming weekend." Taryn's stomach churned. "We've lost so many customers to the Summit Ridge Bakery I need to win."

"One summer fair won't make a big difference."

"It will remind people about Lawson's Bakery. That it's the place to buy bread for dinner, cookies for lunches, and cakes and pies for special occasions and has been for decades."

She could visualize her theme with the Shakespeare title so clearly. Of course, that was because she'd created it ten months ago. Now…

"The fair will give us exposure. The same as the outdoor patio is doing." The other bakery had only a small seating area inside. For two nights, customers had packed her patio. "But starting over with the booth will take time I don't have."

Her shifts, management stuff, life… Something would have to give—likely sleep—for her to finish by Friday.

Jayden added donuts to the top shelf of the case. "Hire someone."

That was one solution, except she needed to cut expenses. "I have to replace all the materials for the new booth. I can't afford to pay someone."

"You're running on fumes." Concern laced each of his words. "You can't keep up this pace."

"That's what coffee is for." It had become her lifeline. She couldn't rely on caffeine indefinitely, but it wouldn't be forever. "I need to do whatever I can over the next three weeks."

He raised a brow. "Before your mom and dad get home?"

She nodded. "They hate change. But neither my parents nor my grandparents faced any competition. If the booth wins, they might see my other ideas for the bakery are solid."

"Could work."

"Will work."

"With that optimistic outlook, it will." His grin spread. "Too bad I'm worthless with power tools. Now, give me a mixer, and I'm your guy."

"That's why you have Rachelle," Taryn teased.

"I married a firefighter for a reason. She's not afraid of heights, either, so she cleans the gutters."

The couple complemented each other well. They didn't worry about gender roles and laughed at stereotypes. They'd been trying to have a baby for years. Taryn hoped that happened for them sooner rather than later. "Lucky."

His gaze softened. Any minute, heart eyes would appear. "Very. It's too bad you don't have a boyfriend who's handy with power tools."

"Yeah, but I'm on a sabbatical from dating."

"It's been what?" He refilled the tray of croissants. "Five months?"

Over six, but who was counting? "I don't have time to date, anyway."

Jayden snickered. "You made time before that hotshot attorney…"

Her jaw clenched, and she balled her hands.

"Garrett Andrews isn't a hotshot." She didn't need some egotistical lawyer, no matter how gorgeous, treating her as a convenience. "He's a jerk."

When Garrett told her he'd call after he left town, she'd believed him. Why wouldn't she when they'd had so much fun together while he was visiting his sister over Christmas? But he'd lied the same as the shed seller. Two important data points she would remember in the future.

Trust needed to be earned, not given freely.

"He ghosted me." Saying the words left a bitter taste in her mouth.

Not because she'd suffered a heartbreak. Oh, being ghosted stung, but mainly because he'd made her feel as if she hadn't measured up somehow. She hated thinking she wasn't enough.

"If Callie didn't mention her three brothers, I'd have no idea if he was alive or dead." Taryn flexed her fingers. She wouldn't let the man affect her.

Jayden added more banana walnut muffins to the case. "Run a search on him."

Taryn cringed. "Too stalkerish for me."

His mouth quirked. "Did you ask his younger sister about him?"

"Nope. And I won't," Taryn blurted.

"Callie still doesn't know you went out?"

"You're the only one who knows." Taryn straightened the menu cards on the counter. "I'd only look foolish mentioning it now, given what happened."

Jayden shook his head. "The way he wanted Callie to have all the attention after she announced her engagement made him seem like a nice guy."

"I fell for it, too. I wish I'd never met him."

"Just because Garrett turned out to be a jerk doesn't mean you should paint all men the same."

Taryn raised her chin. "Have I treated you or the employees differently since December?"

"No."

"Customers?"

"Nope, but you didn't want to date the new paramedic Rachelle introduced you to."

"He was attractive, but he only wanted free baked goods."

"Possibly, but he works with a construction crew on his days off. Go out with him so he can help you."

That appealed to Taryn for a nanosecond. "I would never use someone that way. Besides, I only have a few days to rebuild the booth. I couldn't squeeze in a date, too. But no worries. I'll figure it out."

Jayden made room for more blueberry muffins. "That means you'll do all the work yourself and not sleep for a week. That's what happened with the *Nutcracker*-themed window."

Taryn placed her hand over her heart. "That Christmas window was a masterpiece."

He nodded. "If everyone, including you, hadn't helped redo Callie's doggy daycare window, the bakery would have won for the second year in a row."

"No regrets." The First Avenue Business Association sponsored an annual Christmas window contest. That night, no one had been competing when people came together to decorate Wags and Tails's window in a way none of them would forget. "Callie deserved to win. Hers turned out so special, but the gloves are off for the fair's booth decorating contest. Lawson's Bakery has never won, and this is our year to pull off what my grandparents and parents couldn't."

Jayden didn't appear convinced. "You'll exhaust your-self."

She shrugged. "You know what every baker who works the early shift says."

"Sleep is overrated," they said in unison and then laughed.

"I get by on five hours." That much was true.

"If you want me to take more shifts…"

"You work enough. Unless you need the money, I'll ask someone else."

"Rachelle would prefer me at home on her days off."

"You can cut your hours." That would save Taryn money. She didn't need to be paid overtime on top of what she regularly earned working there.

"I'm happy the way things are. I enjoy running things here. You know, Rachelle is in charge of our family."

Taryn laughed. It was true, but that worked for them.

"Well, you're the best assistant manager an owner could ask for." She meant every word and wanted to give him a raise once the bakery was back on track. "I have no idea how I ended up hiring an all-male staff, but you're better with the other guys than me."

"You do great with everyone, but your baking skills intimidate them."

"I'm as intimidating as a ladybug."

"A ladybug who carries a machete," he joked.

"You mean a spatula."

"Let's just say you set the bar high for people who work here."

Her shoulders drooped. "Not that quality matters to customers if they can save money at the place in Summit Ridge."

Jayden added bagels to the tray. "They've gone overboard with loss leaders."

Loss leaders on what had been her top-selling products. Maybe that was their plan to bring in customers, but each time she created a new product, they did, too. It felt personal. "I don't know how they are making money."

"They can't keep it up for much longer, or they'll go out of business." Jayden grabbed another tray from the tall rolling cart filled with trays of baked goods. "People will be back."

She nodded, trying not to get discouraged. "I keep waiting for someone else to quit and go to work there."

"Stop worrying. Those who wanted to leave took the offers. The rest of us didn't."

Jayden's package had included benefits and the title of manager. Part of her thought he should have taken it, but she was relieved he hadn't. "Thanks for staying."

"We're a team." He bumped his shoulder against hers.

"The others who are still here feel the same way. Things will turn around when the newness of the other place wears off, and they raise prices."

"I hope so."

If not, and if the outdoor patio and exposure from the summer fair didn't bring in more business, Taryn had no idea what she would do.

# Chapter Two

AFTER FLYING INTO Seattle and driving to Silver Falls, Garrett Andrews rolled his suitcase into Margot Winslow's charming two-story house. The wood molding, built-ins, and bright quilts hanging like tapestries provided character. So did her dogs. The pair jumped on his legs, panting and acting as if he were a giant piece of bacon.

A small, tan pup barked.

The sharp sound bounced off the hardwood floor and echoed through the entryway before the door shut with a thud. That didn't quiet...

Sadie and Angus.

Those were their names, but he couldn't remember if Sadie was the smaller, barking dog or if she was the quieter, medium-sized, black and gray one. Whoever was who, they were as loud and as energetic as when he'd visited in December.

The little one placed his front paws on Garrett and barked again. The larger sniffed his shoes before examining his suitcase.

He laughed. "I thought cats were the curious ones."

"Down. Don't bark, Angus." Margot used a firm tone

before patting the dog's head. She glanced up at Garrett. "He gets excited when we have company."

Garrett repeated their names silently, staring at each dog, so he wouldn't forget which was which. Might as well say them out loud. "Angus is fine. Sadie, too."

"It's a good thing I had no children, or they'd be spoiled like these two."

The dogs didn't settle.

Angus barked.

"Oh, sweet boy." With her long, flowing skirt, knitted tunic, a patchwork, knee-length quilted vest, and a single braid reaching her waist, she reminded him of an Earth Mother type. Only her gray hair suggested she might be in her sixties, not fifties. "You remember Garrett. He's one of Callie's brothers. That makes him family."

Almost family, but no reason to quibble since the wedding between her nephew, Brandt Winslow, and Garrett's sister, Callie, was a week from Saturday.

He didn't know if aunt-in-law was an official term, but Margot took the role seriously based on the "nephew" birthday card he received from her in April. "Just wait until my two brothers arrive next week. Little Angus won't know what to do."

"He'll enjoy the company."

"Thanks for letting us stay here. Callie's cottage is cute, but it was too crowded at Christmastime. I can't imagine being there with the wedding prep."

"You mean stress. None of you would have any fun. Now that Angus has settled, let me welcome you properly."

Margot hugged Garrett before motioning to his left hand. "How is a handsome lawyer like you still single?"

He shrugged. "I haven't met the right woman."

Margot's blue-eyed gaze narrowed. "Most likely, you haven't found a woman more interesting than your work."

"True." Garrett remembered what Brandt had told him. "Is this where I'm supposed to tell you not to play matchmaker?"

Margot placed her hand over her heart, feigning innocence. "Who, me?"

Garrett laughed. "I'm a trial attorney, remember? I know all the moves and tells, so don't pretend with me."

"My nephew is spinning yarns."

Sadie nudged him with her nose, and he petted her head. "The evidence suggests you take the Fifth or plead guilty."

"Don't go all lawyer on me, Garrett Andrews." Margot picked up Angus. "There are several lovely single women who would catch your eye if you look up from your phone."

"I'm sure there are." One popped into his mind. Garrett rubbed his neck. Now wasn't the time to think about Taryn Lawson. "But there's a reason your matchmaking won't work. I live in L.A. and spend at least eighty hours a week at my office or in the courtroom. Relationships are hard even when I live in the same city as someone."

"A little vacation romance wouldn't hurt."

Hadn't he said the same thing in December? At least he and Taryn hadn't been interested in anything more than hanging out over the holidays. "Yes, but what if it turned into something more? A long-distance relationship would be impossible."

"If you met the right person, you could make it work."

Brandt was correct about his aunt. She wanted everyone paired up. "Please don't arrange any blind dates or accidental meetings or whatever else you do to fix up people."

Margot pouted. "You're no fun."

He laughed. "I'm not. I'm also a partner in a big L.A. law firm, so my life is there. I can't uproot if I fall for some small-town girl who plans on living and dying in Silver Falls. Another reason not to play matchmaker. But Keaton's house-sitting for Callie while she's on her honeymoon. I'm sure he'd love to meet women while he's in town."

His younger brother would kill him, but a summer romance was precisely what the serious professor needed.

Mischief gleamed in her gaze. She shifted Angus to her other hip. "Oh, yes. I know the perfect woman for him."

Better Keaton than Garrett. "I'm sure you do."

Margot wagged a finger. "It's your turn the next time you're in town."

That wouldn't be for a while, but… "What about Flynn?"

"I've been trying to figure out who would make the best wife for a surgeon." She sounded perplexed.

Garrett laughed, but she would soon realize what the entire family knew. Flynn might never find a woman who measured up to his exacting standards. "I'm sure you'll come up with someone, eventually."

"Oh, I will." Margot motioned to the stairs. "Since you're the first here, you can choose which guest room you want. Each has the door open and towels at the end of the bed. Pick whichever one appeals to you."

"Callie mentioned this would be like staying in a B&B only with a doting innkeeper and three delicious meals a day."

Margot brushed off his words before setting Angus on the floor. "My manager does a wonderful job at the quilt shop, so I've cut my hours. Having people around will be fun. Otherwise, this big house gets too quiet with just me, Sadie, and Angus."

"Well, I appreciate it."

"Do you have many plans while you're here?"

"I have some work to do, but I came early in case Callie needed help." Though the real reason he was there was to keep from losing his vacation. He'd accrued too much, even after spending two weeks in Silver Falls over the holidays.

"Your sister's to-do list grows by the day."

"Happy to lend a hand, especially since Flynn and Keaton won't be here for a few more days."

"There will be plenty for your brothers to do once they arrive."

"If I know Callie and my mom, you're right." That reminded Garrett. "If you need anything while I'm here…"

"Now that you mention it." Margot reached into her vest pocket and removed a piece of paper. "I'm making dinner for your family tonight. Would you mind picking up a few items so I can concentrate on cooking?"

"Sure." His suitcase was in the way. "Let me put my bag upstairs, and then I'll get whatever's on your list."

"Thank you." Margot's blue eyes twinkled. "I love that I'm gaining a niece and three more nephews. More people to run my errands."

"That's one way to look at it."

"And more to buy Christmas presents for."

He laughed. "That's another."

Garrett carried his suitcase to the second floor. He took the bedroom farthest from the bathroom, which had a queen-sized four-poster bed. Two towels, a hand towel, and washcloths sat on a beautiful quilt, most likely sewn by Margot.

As he changed into shorts and a T-shirt, a bird sang outside his window. The cheerful tune brought a smile to his face. He peered out, not seeing anything but branches and leaves in the tall maple tree. He hoped the bird came back.

Garrett returned downstairs. "What do you need me to get?"

Margot handed him the list and a large canvas tote bag. "There are a few stops, but I only need an item or two from each place, so if you feel like walking, you can."

"I could use the exercise after the flight and drive." As he read over the list, his gaze zeroed in on one line.

*Two loaves of artisan bread from Lawson's Bakery.*

His breath hitched. An image of Taryn's pretty smile and adorable dimples formed in his mind. He'd had a valid reason for not contacting her in January, but he was here for two weeks. Maybe they could reconnect.

"See something interesting?" Margot asked.

Garrett kept his expression neutral. Something he'd

learned to do working in the DA's office before striking out on his own. He didn't want her to guess he'd been thinking about Taryn. "A few things."

"Well, the oven timer is about to buzz. Off you go."

He folded the list, tucked it into his shorts pocket, and held on to the tote bag. "Have fun cooking."

As he walked toward First Avenue, the sun beat down on him. He put on his sunglasses.

When he reached the strip of businesses, Garrett stopped. The town was no longer decked for the holidays. Instead of garland and wreaths, flower baskets hung from the old-fashioned-looking streetlamps. People strolled in and out of buildings. Two women pushed strollers as a kid rode past them on a skateboard.

Silver Falls was nothing like downtown L.A. where he lived in a high-rise condo. But the slower, quieter pace of the small town appealed to him on a gut level. Not as a place to live permanently, but he enjoyed visiting.

Garrett stared up the street. He could go one of two ways—hit the shops on the right side first or cross the road to the left. If Garrett stayed on this side, the bakery would be his last stop. He didn't know if Taryn would be interested in picking up where they left off, but perhaps they could grab a drink or a meal together.

Flutters filled his stomach.

He hadn't felt those since…December.

That made Garrett's decision an easy one. He stayed on the right side of the street.

He picked up two pounds of beans at the coffee shop.

The small sample of iced coffee refreshed him, so that he could hit the next place. Two yards of fabric was waiting for him at Margot's quilt shop. The liquor store had one champagne and two wine bottles for Margot. A good thing he had the tote bag, or he would have been juggling too many shopping bags. He purchased batteries from the hardware store. A jar of salad dressing from the Falls Café came next.

He studied Margot's list. Only one stopped remained— Lawson's Bakery.

As he opened the door, a bell dinged. Not the jingling he remembered. The smell, however, hadn't changed. The mouthwatering aroma of baking bread tickled his nose. He would order something, or he'd never survive until dinner-time.

The tables were empty. That surprised him, given how crowded the place was the last time he was there. The pleasant weather might be the culprit, or people ordering to go.

Garrett approached the counter. He hadn't taken three steps when Taryn stepped out from the kitchen.

She wore all-white clothes with a hairnet and cap. Six months had passed, but she looked the same. No, that wasn't entirely true. She was prettier than Garrett remembered. He waited for her light-up-his-life grin to appear.

Her gaze met his, and her eyes widened. "Garrett?"

Her voice was tentative...surprised.

He got that. They hadn't seen each other in months. "Hey. Margot sent me by for two loaves of your artisan bread."

"She phoned in the order and prepaid."

Taryn grabbed a bag from under the counter and handed it to him. She moved so fast he almost dropped it.

But a whiff of Taryn's sugary scent brought memories of her sweet kiss to the surface. Yes, getting together sounded better and better.

Garrett added the bread to the tote. It barely fit.

"Thanks." He flashed his most charming smile, the one that worked as well with the women on a jury as it did at a party. "I'm in town for Callie's wedding. I'll be here for two weeks."

Taryn raised a brow and pressed her lips together.

She must want him to ask her out. That was fine with him. He'd start with something easy so that they could catch up. Then he would invite her for a meal. "Let's meet for coffee tomorrow."

Her eyebrows furrowed. "Seriously?"

He nodded. "Tea Leaves and Coffee Beans. Say three, unless you can't take off. I have a few things to do but have a flexible schedule. The same as the last time I was here."

Not exactly subtle, but at least she would know where he was coming from.

Her jaw tensed. Lines deepened on her forehead. "I don't believe this."

Her harsh tone surprised him. "What?"

Taryn's lips thinned. "You have some nerve, waltzing in here as if you hadn't ghosted me over six months ago."

He stiffened. They'd agreed to keep in touch but made no promises. Neither of them wanted a relationship, so he didn't know where her anger came from. "I had a reason—"

"Save it for someone who cares. I'm not stupid enough to fall for a made-up excuse now that you're in town and want to pick up where we left off." She stared down her nose. "I'm not interested in a selfish man who is only after something convenient for him. Forget having coffee. I'd rather not see you again."

Each word hit like a slap to his face. He didn't understand her reaction. Okay, he might have handled things better in January, but she acted as if he'd dumped her. "Look, I get you're upset, but we never said we were girlfriend and boyfriend. I had a good reason not to call you. There was—"

"Do you want anything else?" she interrupted.

He wanted to apologize, but she appeared too upset to listen. "I'd like a molasses cookie, please."

"I'll have Jayden get that for you. One moment." She disappeared into the kitchen.

A minute later, Jayden came out, pulling on plastic gloves. The baker had always been friendly, joking around and wearing a big grin. Today, his expression was pinched and his eyes dark.

"How are you?" Garrett asked.

"One molasses cookie coming up." Jayden placed a cookie in a small paper bag. "Here you go."

Garrett jockeyed the bags to remove his wallet. "How much?"

Jayden glanced over his shoulder, but no one was there. "On the house."

"Taryn's upset."

"That's putting it mildly."

"I tried to explain."

Jayden rolled his eyes before crossing his arms over his chest. "You're a lawyer. You should be smart enough to realize it's too late."

Garrett didn't want to leave without explaining, but he might have to wait. He shoved a five-dollar bill in the tip jar. He was here for two weeks—plenty of time to explain.

As he opened the bakery's door, the bell rang again.

"Is he gone?" Taryn's voice sounded shaky.

Tension drew his shoulder blades together. Garrett had never heard her speak that way. He forced himself not to glance back to make sure she was okay. But he didn't need a visual cue to know she wasn't.

He was the reason, even if it made no sense to him. Okay, he'd ghosted her, but Taryn should have let him explain why. Instead, she made it clear he wasn't welcome.

Fine.

He would keep his distance.

Silver Falls was small, but how hard would it be to avoid the bakery and her while he was in town?

What was that phrase Taryn always used?

Easy-peasy.

# Chapter Three

A s GARRETT SAT at Margot's dining room table, the conversation bounced like ping-pong balls from one topic to another. Brandt and Callie updated everyone on the wedding, and their heart eyes would make a lesser man gag. But seeing his little sister so happy pleased Garrett.

His father wiped his mouth with a napkin. He appeared to enjoy the meal and the company. Not once had he glanced at his cell phone during dinner. That had to be a record.

"Pass the bread, please," his father said.

Garrett handed him the plate full of warm-from-the-oven slices. He hadn't taken a piece. Based on the hurt in Taryn's eyes and voice, her feelings for him had changed since December. The signs had been there from the start. No expertise in body language, facial expressions, tells, and vocal tone needed.

And it sucked.

His appetite waning as the uncomfortable knot in his stomach grew, Garrett pushed food on his plate, so no one noticed he wasn't eating. He was a good person, not like other jerks in L.A. who messed around and broke hearts as if it were a game of pool. He'd never been that guy at his fraternity or in law school. Sure, he dated a lot, keeping things casual, but he respected women and never wanted karma to get him via Callie.

Flirty kisses to heated ones aside, Garrett believed he and Taryn were on the same page about what they were and weren't in December.

His throat went from Death Valley dry to Sahara Desert parched.

He bypassed the wine for his glass of ice water and drank.

It didn't help.

Garrett needed to take action. Taryn had sidelined him by refusing to listen. All he wanted to do was make her feel better. She would the second he explained why he'd never contacted her.

He sipped more water.

Should he let it go as Taryn wanted?

His mother held her fork in mid-air. "The meal is delicious, Margot. Thanks for having us over."

"It is." Callie leaned over the table. "I'm so happy you're in charge of the rehearsal dinner."

Brandt nodded. "One less thing to worry about."

"It's my pleasure." Margot raised her glass at the couple before focusing on Brandt. "Your parents were relieved not having to coordinate something from Oregon."

The conversation continued, but the words flew right over Garrett. Maybe he should rethink drinking more wine.

Margot eyed his plate. "You haven't eaten much, Garrett."

He forced a bite of the roast beef, not wanting to draw attention to his lack of appetite.

"Lawson's Bakery makes the best bread," his dad said, reaching for another slice.

"Everything they make is wonderful." Callie's face glowed—the definition of a radiant bride. "Taryn is baking our wedding cake. It's going to be amazing. I had no idea how to pick flavors during our tasting. They were all delicious."

Brandt laughed. "Which is why we're having more cakes than bridesmaids or groomsmen."

Callie made a face. "It's called a groom's cake."

"One might be," he teased. "But three?"

"Anything goes at weddings," Margot chimed in.

"I agree." His mom raised a glass of red wine. "Callie gets whatever she wants. That's how weddings work."

Margot nodded. "Hear, hear."

"That's why Rex will be the ring bearer." Brandt announced with an I'm-so-in-love gleam in his eyes. "A dog in the wedding party is the perfect addition."

His mother's face paled. Her mouth slanted. "I—"

"Rex will be a great ring bearer," his dad interrupted.

*Way to go, Dad.* But Garrett didn't feel like laughing with Taryn still on his mind.

"Thanks, Dad." Callie shimmied her shoulders. "You should see Rex's bow tie. He'll look adorable. Almost as good as Brandt."

"I'm sure he'll be more handsome." Brandt kissed her

cheek before looking at everyone else with an amused gaze. "I've accepted Rex is her true love, but I don't mind being second. He was in her life long before I was."

"I love you both. My first true love with four feet is Rex, and the honor of being my first true love with two feet belongs to you." As she stared at Brandt, love radiated from her to him. "Just think, if I'd become a veterinarian instead of buying Wags and Tails, we might never have met."

Their mother lowered her wineglass. "True, but you would have made a wonderful vet."

Callie's lips pressed together in a thin line, but she didn't lower her gaze or cringe as she had in the past. This time, she sat tall with her chin lifted. "We'll never know."

"And that's okay," their mom added. "You're where you should be."

His sister's grin returned, brighter than ever. "I am."

Garrett released the breath he'd been holding. His parents finally understood how their expectations had hurt Callie. He and his brothers—all type A personalities—hadn't helped matters. A good thing she'd spoken up in December, or who knows how this wedding would have gone?

As Brandt shifted in his chair, his gaze never strayed from Callie for long. "This dinner was what I needed after a day full of meetings and phone calls with investors. Though I overate."

His future brother-in-law had founded one company, consulted for several years, and started a new venture to develop apps earlier this year. The guy was intelligent and driven, but Brandt's devotion to Callie impressed Garrett the most.

"Then, my plan for a walk and dessert will work out perfectly." Margot rubbed her hands together. "The bakery's patio is finally open. I thought we'd eat there."

Garrett's stomach dropped. If he didn't know better, he would think it hit the floor with a thundering splat. "Do we need dessert after such a delicious meal? I'm full."

Brandt nodded. "Same, but I can squeeze in a brownie. And anything to stick it to my former best friend and business partner, who's involved in a competing bakery in Summit Ridge."

Nope. It was not happening on Garrett's watch. He would suggest an alternative plan. That was one of his strengths. He'd kept him and Taryn secret so it wouldn't take away from Callie and Brandt's engagement. He wasn't about to announce they'd gone out now, which he would have to do, if he admitted Taryn didn't want to see him again. No, this was best for her and his sister.

"I say we open another bottle of wine and enjoy the company and the air-conditioning here." He raised his nearly empty wineglass. "That way, we don't have to fight the crowds."

"And not have dessert?" Eyebrows furrowed, Callie leaned toward him. "Who are you, and what have you done with my brother?"

Garrett's shoulders bunched. "What do you mean?"

"Well, dear." His mother patted his hand. "You have a sweet tooth. Otherwise, you wouldn't have gone to the bakery every day in December."

He enjoyed sweets, but that wasn't why he'd been there. Though, Taryn's kisses were warm and sugary like the desserts she baked. Not that his family knew that.

Garrett gulped. "It was Christmastime."

"No matter what season, it's always time for dessert." Callie licked her lips. "And you love chocolate almost as much as I do."

True, but... "I enjoy chocolate. You can't love things."

"Except your job," his dad joked. "Right, son?"

Garrett forced a laugh. His dad was a partner at one of the biggest law firms in Southern California and a workaholic like the rest of them, including Garrett's mom, a doctor. The only exception was Callie, which proved she was the smartest of the bunch. "Right."

Callie jumped to her feet. "So let's go."

Garrett remained seated, even though he was the only one left at the table. He fought the urge to hold on to the chair so no one could drag him away. "I have work to catch up on."

"You're on vacation. I'm not taking no for an answer." Callie grabbed his arm before pulling him to his feet. "Come with us, or I'll turn into a bridezilla."

Brandt cringed. "No one wants that to happen. Please, Garrett, our fate until the wedding lies in your hands."

Not really.

He wanted to do the right thing for Taryn and himself.

Still, his family's expectant gazes weakened his resolve, but he didn't want to take away the spotlight on Callie and Brandt. "There might have been a misunderstanding with

Taryn earlier."

"When you picked up the bread?" Margot's eyebrows drew together. "I paid ahead of time."

"It was no big deal," he backtracked, not wanting to take the focus off Callie.

His sister placed her hands on her hips. "So there's no reason for you not to go."

If Taryn were working, maybe she wouldn't go out on the patio and even realize he was there. "Fine, I'll go, but that means no bridezilla tantrums from you."

"Yay. And you know I'm not the tantrum-throwing type." Callie bounced on her toes the way she'd done since she was little, even though she was all grown-up and getting married.

His chest tightened, squeezing his heart tightly. Brandt had better treat Callie right, or he'd be dealing with Garrett, Flynn, and Keaton. No one would hurt their baby sister.

*Ugh.* The truth smacked into Garrett like a judge's gavel.

No wonder Jayden acted protective earlier. Taryn didn't have any brothers, but she had her staff.

Garrett respected that, but he wasn't trying to hurt Taryn. That was why he wanted to keep his distance. As long as she didn't see him, everything would be okay. "Okay, let's go."

IT WAS ANOTHER busy night at the bakery. Taryn placed an éclair on a plate. She didn't have to force a cheery mood. Not when tables on the patio and inside were packed on a

Monday night.

*This will work.*

Taryn wiggled her toes before handing the dessert to a smiling customer. "Enjoy your éclair."

For the first time that evening, no one stepped up to the counter. The lull let her take a break and a sip of water.

"They keep coming tonight," Jayden whispered. "Not complaining, but we might need to add a person to this shift."

Excellent customer service made a difference, according to Grandpa. But Taryn wouldn't hire someone until she saw the numbers.

"If business keeps up next week, I'll see who wants extra hours temporarily. If we sustain this level, we can make it permanent through summer." Taryn removed her gloves. "You've worked long enough today. Go home to your lovely wife."

"She's on duty, and you need the help."

Taryn recognized Callie coming from the back entrance and waved. "As soon as I can afford it, you're getting a raise."

"Good, because I deserve one." With a wink, he headed into the kitchen.

Taryn smiled. "Welcome to Lawson's Bakery."

Callie's complexion glowed. "The patio is amazing."

"Thank you." Taryn acknowledged Brandt and Margot, but she didn't recognize the couple with them. The man, however, looked vaguely familiar. "I'm so happy with how it turned out."

"The customers like it too," Margot said.

As Taryn's chest swelled with pride, she nodded. Now, all she needed was for her parents to acknowledge it. "That's the best part."

"Your brownies are the best." Brandt stepped forward, putting his arm around Callie. "But the patio is a close second."

"I don't think you've met my parents, Tina and John Andrews." Callie glanced at the man and woman. "Mom and Dad, this is Taryn Lawson, who makes the tastiest baked goods in the Pacific Northwest, if not the West Coast."

"We ate a few of your desserts over Christmas, but tonight was our first time tasting your bread. Delicious."

A thrill shot through Taryn. She stood taller. "Thanks. What can I get you?"

As they studied the evening specials on the board behind her, she readied her hand on the cash register. One by one, they ordered.

"Is that everything?" Taryn asked before she hit total.

"We should get Garrett something." Margot's voice softened. "He's a sweetheart for sitting outside with the dogs."

*Wait.* Was Garrett there? Taryn's muscles bunched. She hadn't expected him to return. Not when she'd told him she never wanted to see him again. Rude, yes, but given how he made her feel about herself... Still, the nerve of him coming tonight sent her blood boiling.

"Garrett loves molasses cookies," Callie chimed in. "Isn't that right, Taryn?"

Her hands balled. "Your brother had a cookie earlier. He doesn't get a second one."

33

Callie startled.

Margot's jaw dropped.

Brandt blew out a breath.

Mr. and Mrs. Andrews shared a look.

Taryn's hands shook, but she didn't care. Muscle memory allowed her to fill the order, and what common sense remained kept her from holding any baked good too hard. She didn't glance up.

Instead, she moved like a robot, each motion programmed in and no extra steps. Plates sat on a tray. So did the drinks. She rang up the sale and even remembered to give two dog biscuits shaped like bones to Margot. "For Angus and Sadie."

"Thanks, dear." Concern filled Margot's eyes.

*Please don't ask.* Taryn pushed the tray forward on the counter. That was when she noticed Callie was missing. Probably off to warn her brother about the crazy baker who wouldn't give him a cookie.

She plastered on a smile that was probably more deranged clown than cheerful. "Have a nice evening."

Thankfully, no one else stepped up to order. Taryn hurried into the kitchen.

"Brecken," she called to the rising high school senior. "Please take the front."

He left the loaves of bread he was wrapping. "Sure thing, Boss."

She headed to her office, plopped into her chair, and buried her face in her hands. "What is wrong with you?"

"I was about to ask you the same question." Jayden

touched her shoulder. "You, okay?"

Yes. No. She had no idea. "I made a fool of myself in front of Callie, Brandt, and their families."

"Fool isn't in your vocabulary."

"It was tonight. And my picture is now being sent to dictionaries everywhere—online or print."

"It can't be that bad."

Heat pooled in Taryn's cheeks. "I told Callie her brother couldn't have a cookie."

Jayden's jaw jutted forward. "He's back?"

"That was my reaction."

"That egotistical lawyer is the only fool."

Taryn's pulse rate returned to normal. "Thanks. I've never gotten so angry like that."

"The guy triggered you. It happens."

"I can't believe this happened in front of customers, especially Callie and Margot."

"They'll understand."

"But they have no idea what's been going on."

"That's okay. This isn't like you, but his appearance set you reeling, and Callie caught you off-guard." Jayden sat on the edge of her desk. "So this thing with Garrett really affected you?"

"I wasn't in love with him." The words poured from her lips faster than runny ganache.

Jayden raised an eyebrow. His look suggested he didn't believe her. "I didn't say you were, but love at first sight is real. That's how it was with Rachelle and me."

"It wasn't like that with us. Garrett and I had fun. We

were getting closer, so I'd hoped it might turn into more eventually, but neither of us wanted a long-distance relationship. But when he ghosted me, it magnified how I was already feeling. Today and tonight brought up the emotions again."

"About what?" Jayden asked.

"That I'm not enough. My parents keep implying I'm not smart enough to keep the bakery going, even though I've been doing it for years. Then, I wasn't enough for Garrett to call me after he left, when he said he would. Now, given the downturn in business, I wonder if my mom and dad are right. And I don't need Garrett Andrews reaffirming it for me."

Jayden rubbed his neck. "That's a lot to unpack."

"It's me, not Garrett. I'm taking out my emotions and insecurity on him." She clasped her hands to keep from fidgeting. "Does that break it down for you better?"

"Yes, but love at first sight exists. That would explain why you took being ghosted so hard."

"It would in a romantic, tragic movie of the week way, but a broken heart isn't why I overreacted." A heartbreak might be easier to deal with, too. "I… I hate being disregarded."

Especially when her parents did the same thing to her.

"Fine. You're not in love with him." Jayden sounded relieved. "But Garrett's in town, he's your friend's brother, and there aren't many places to hide in Silver Falls. What are you going to do?"

Taryn wished she knew. Taking a vacation or locking

herself in her house for two weeks weren't options. She had a booth to build, desserts to bake, and a hundred other things on her to-do list. "Get over it."

And pray she didn't see Garrett Andrews anytime soon.

# Chapter Four

HOLDING ON TO the two dog leashes, Garrett sat at a table in the patio area with Angus and Sadie. He'd offered to stay outside with the dogs while the others headed inside to order in case Taryn was working tonight. The place was packed, but if things went his way, he wouldn't see her.

It was almost eight, and the sun was still out. Customers spoke over contemporary music playing from hidden speakers. People smiled and laughed. The mood was light, but a weight pressed against his shoulders.

*Leave.*

He wanted to return to Margot's house and pretend he hadn't upset Taryn. But Callie and his parents would have questions if he took off. Too bad the dogs were behaving themselves, or he would use them as an excuse to get out of there.

"Bark or something," he whispered.

Sadie and Angus stared at him with hopeful gazes and wagging tails. They didn't make a peep nor pull against their leashes. *Of course, now the little one behaves.*

"Sorry, dogs." He held out his free hand. "I've got nothing. I don't carry treats in my pocket."

Sadie tilted her head as if she understood him. As Angus panted, his tail sped up.

Girl versus boy.

Garrett didn't feel like laughing, though. It was him, not the bakery. The patio's vibe was comfortable and welcoming. Strands of globe lights and flower baskets hanging from the pergola set the mood. Trellises with vines and fairy lights added a theme park feel.

Tasteful, not kitschy.

The little touches, especially the wooden signs painted with desserts and their names, had Taryn written all over them. Her creativity extended beyond baked goods. It showed in the bakery's design, the new patio, and her one-story home.

Only a small table for two was empty. The new addition appeared to be a success. Good for her and the bakery.

Not that Garrett could congratulate Taryn. Emailing or sending a card was probably a bad idea. Maybe when he was home he would write her and explain what happened. That might be the only way to prove his innocence. Though she might not read whatever he sent.

He slumped. "I'm in the doghouse, guys."

Sadie and Angus watched him.

Garrett half laughed. "Puppy dog eyes? That's all you've got for me?"

Footsteps sounded.

His sister marched toward him with pursed lips and a tight expression.

"This doesn't look good," he whispered to the dogs.

Sadie rubbed her muzzle against his leg.

"Garrett Robert Andrews." Flames danced in Callie's eyes. Her arms flew to her waist, so her elbows stuck out. It was the same position their mom took when upset. "What did you do to Taryn?"

*Uh-oh.* Garrett gulped. "I told you I didn't want to come."

"You said there might have been a slight misunderstanding. An understatement?"

Not knowing what happened inside the bakery, he shrugged.

"I asked Taryn if you usually liked molasses cookies, and she said you couldn't have a cookie. Taryn has never said anything like that, and she wasn't joking. What did you do?"

His muscles tensed, not that they'd relaxed much since he arrived. "Is she okay?"

"I don't know. I left to come out here." Callie dragged her teeth over her lower lip before glancing at the door to the bakery. "What's going on?"

His temple throbbed, threatening to explode into a massive headache. He massaged his forehead with his free hand. "It's a long story."

"I've got all night."

Which meant she wouldn't let this go. No one appeared to be paying attention to them. He didn't want to drag Callie into any drama or small-town gossip. Taryn, either. But he would keep his voice low, just in case someone eavesdropped. "This isn't the place to—"

"Taryn is my friend. She's baking our wedding cake."

Lines formed on Callie's forehead and around her mouth. "If you've caused a problem…"

"Taryn got upset at me when I picked up the bread earlier. She said she'd rather not see me again."

"I must be missing something. You haven't been here since December."

Garrett brushed his hand through his hair. He didn't see a way out of this except by telling the truth. "Taryn and I went out when I was here the last time."

Callie blinked as if she were trying to make sense of what he'd said. "One date shouldn't be that big of a deal."

No, but… He swallowed.

"It was more than once." Garrett blew out a breath, only none of his tension left. His muscles tightened into marbles, making his skin itch. Might as well say it. "Taryn and I saw each other every day after we met, except for Christmas Day."

He'd tried to think of a way to be with Taryn then, too, but his absence on a holiday would have made his family suspicious, so he'd called her instead.

"But…" Callie's eyebrows drew together. "You never mentioned it. Neither did she."

"I asked her not to."

"Why?"

"That was when you told us you didn't think you fit into the family. That you felt overshadowed by me, Flynn, and Keaton." Sadie nudged his leg, and he patted her. At least the dog appreciated him. "You and Brandt were newly engaged. It was your time to be the center of the attention."

"I wouldn't have minded."

"Stop thinking about what's happening now and go back to what it would have been like in December." He wanted Callie to understand his reasoning. "Mom would have gone on about two relationships, not just your engagement, and Dad would have given both of us his spiel about the importance of prenups and a family discount at the firm."

Callie rubbed her lips together. "Mom and Dad probably would have told us to have a double wedding to save time and money."

Okay, his sister got it. Garrett released the breath he'd been holding. "Exactly."

"But if dating Taryn was important to you—"

"It wasn't." The words rushed from Garrett's mouth. Callie was a romantic at heart. He didn't want her to think he and Taryn had been serious. "Our time together hinted at the possibility of more, but neither of us wanted a relationship."

"You guys ended things before you left for L.A.?"

This was the hard part. Being secretive had backfired on him and hurt Taryn. "Not exactly."

"What does that mean?"

Garrett braced himself. He hated disappointing anyone, but especially Callie. "I planned to stay in touch because we got along and enjoyed talking to each other, but then I received those death threats, so I didn't call her. And it wasn't just her. I wasn't in touch with anyone except the family. I wouldn't chance someone coming after my family, friends, or the woman I'd dated over the holidays."

Callie's mouth slanted, her gaze narrowing. "You used a burner phone to keep in touch with us. You could have let Taryn know what was going on."

Yes, but he hadn't been thinking about that. All he'd thought about were the...threats. He blinked, not wanting to be drawn back into the time, but that reminded him of why he hadn't called Taryn. "I didn't want to frighten her."

"You don't know how she would have reacted."

"I don't, but we weren't in a relationship, so why drag her into the mess?"

"You could have called her after things settled down."

Another good point, but Callie hadn't been there. Looking back with hindsight was easier than living through it. He'd questioned so much about his career and life at that point. Garrett rubbed his chest. His heart thumped beneath his palm. "By the time they arrested the perp, it was March. Too late to pick up where we'd left off with a new and fledgling friendship."

Callie's lips parted. "You ghosted her."

"For her safety."

"So, she has no idea death threats were made against you and the people you care about?"

"I tried to tell Taryn today, but she didn't want to listen."

"Of course not." Callie's voice rose an octave. "Let me guess. You strutted into her bakery as if nothing had happened six months ago."

He squirmed. "I didn't strut, but guilty as charged."

Her jaw jutted forward. "What were you thinking?"

Garrett shrugged. "That it was no big deal."

To him, it hadn't been.

Callie groaned. "It's a huge deal, and I'm not even involved. Poor Taryn."

"We weren't head over heels for each other. We live in different states and work long hours where taking time off is rare. We had fun together, but we both knew this would never be more than a holiday romance."

Callie stared at him as if he'd grown a unicorn horn. "That's your defense?"

He nodded.

She leaned toward him. "And Taryn felt the same way as you?"

He started to nod but then shrugged. "She never said differently, though her reaction today makes me wonder."

Callie muttered idiot under her breath. "Taryn would go along with whatever you wanted. She's not a rock-the-boat type but goes with the flow. Most guys get fed up with her work schedule after the second date. She holds her feelings close, which is why when I moved to town, I thought she was standoffish and stuck up. I was wrong."

Garrett's jokes had loosened her up. The more they talked, the less he relied on humor to break the ice. "I never meant to hurt her, but it's not my fault. She's the one who wouldn't listen to me earlier."

"Don't blame Taryn." Callie poked her index finger, sharp and accusing, against his chest. "This is all your fault. I love you, and you're a good guy, but you screwed up. Big-time."

"Don't mince words, sis."

"There's more I want to say, but we're in public." Callie glanced around. "Taryn hasn't been herself lately. I thought it was competition from the new bakery in Summit Ridge, but you must be a part of it, too."

Garrett might be known for his courtroom theatrics and charming a jury, but he was at a loss for words. Totally unlike him. "I'm sorry."

"I'm not the one who needs to hear you say that. Apologize to her."

"I told you. I tried."

"Try again." Callie raised her chin. "Taryn is not only baking our cake, but she's also invited to the wedding. Fix this, so neither of you is uncomfortable. But most especially her. Because this is all on you, bro."

She was right. He sighed. "I'll fix it."

"Now."

"I don't want to upset her more."

Callie's face scrunched. "So you'd rather Taryn didn't sleep tonight?"

"You don't know—"

"Neither do you."

Their family walked toward them. His dad carried a tray of drinks, and Brandt held one with desserts.

"I won't say a word about what happened." Callie kept her voice low. "But only if you go talk to Taryn."

Garrett prided himself on being thorough with every case, whether he was the client's attorney or brought in as a consultant. No matter the circumstances, he gave a hundred and ten percent, even if it meant long days and sleepless nights. He would rather stand in front of a hostile jury with a lifetime prison sentence hanging in the balance than face Taryn right now. He hadn't been this on edge since he asked Lyric Quinn to the senior prom in front of the entire high school.

Still, Callie was correct. He should get this over with before things got more out of hand. He gave the dog leashes to his sister. "I won't be long."

"Take your time and do it right."

"You sound like Mom."

"Finally." Callie beamed.

Garrett wiped his clammy palms over his shorts. "This won't go as well as you think it will."

"I'm an optimist."

"And I'm a realist." Still, he hoped Taryn listened to him.

As he headed toward the door, his dad raised two glasses of iced tea. "You're going the wrong way."

"I'll be right back." At least Garrett hoped so.

As soon as he entered the bakery, the scents of sugary goodness surrounded him. If only his words would melt Taryn's anger as fast as her baked goods disappeared.

Jayden stood behind the counter. His dark gaze sharpened. "Guess I gave lawyers too much credit for being intelligent."

The guy was only looking out for his friend and boss, but that didn't keep Garrett from squaring his shoulders. "I need to speak to Taryn."

A muscle ticked at Jayden's jaw. "Not a good idea to-night."

That was the out he needed, but that wouldn't fly with his sister. Or him, if he were being honest with himself. He hadn't made a name for himself by taking the easy cases. "Callie told me what happened."

"Stay away."

"Too late." Garrett wouldn't declare his innocence. He'd been the catalyst. "I want to apologize. Can I see her? Please."

Jayden hesitated. "I thought you were a good guy and good for her, but the way you ghosted her and then just show up as if it was nothing was harsh, man."

Garrett held up his hands, palms facing out. "I'm not trying to cause trouble or hurt her. But I messed up, and I need to explain why I never called."

Jayden's gaze traveled from Garrett to the hallway lead-ing to the bathroom and office.

"Taryn's had a rough year." Jayden wiped his cheek with his forearm. "Maybe hearing your reason will help her move on, so she can focus on more important issues."

Garrett read between the lines. The same way he did with clients. Taryn was in some kind of trouble. "What's going on?"

Jayden's nostrils flared. "You lost the right to know any-thing when you blew her off."

"I—"

"Stop." The word came out sharp. "I'm not the one who needs or wants to hear your excuse."

Not an excuse. "Can I see her?"

"She's in the office."

Okay, now Garrett was getting somewhere. "Thanks."

"Don't thank me yet. You make her cry…"

His jaw tensed. "If I do, I'll deserve whatever you want to do to me."

IN THE OFFICE, Taryn sat at the desk, staring at the calendar hanging on the wall. The beautiful photographs of baked goods inspired her to create new products. Now, she hoped July's fruit torte calmed her. As she focused on the image, the creamy custard filling slowed her pulse rate, and the bright colors of the fruit relaxed the tight facial muscles. She inhaled, taking the time to fill her lungs to the brim, before exhaling. The boiling of her blood cooled to a simmer.

*Progress.*

Taryn should go to the kitchen, but her bottom remained glued in the chair. She'd made a fool out of herself in front of customers, and that would take her a few more minutes—or longer—to get over.

She kept staring at the calendar.

Maybe she should add another torte to the menu. Hers was popular, but the Summit Ridge Bakery had added an almost identical one to their menu. A second flavor of filling might appeal to customers and differentiate Lawson's from the competition.

The office door opened.

Taryn didn't look over her shoulder. "I'll be out in a minute, Jayden."

"It's not Jayden."

Garrett's voice slithered along her spine. Chills followed. Her hands balled into fists.

*What's he doing here?*

"Are you okay?" Concern sounded in his voice.

All she wanted was for him to leave. "I'm fine."

Not a lie. She would be—eventually.

"Can we talk?" he asked.

"Now isn't a good time." She kept her voice steady, even though her insides twisted worse than a silicone fondant rope mold.

"There probably won't be one."

She would give him that, but that didn't mean she had to speak with him.

Callie called Garrett the egotistical attorney, but the doggy daycare owner was proud of her second oldest brother. Taryn had never seen the cocky side of him but hearing him describe his work showed his stubborn streak. He fought relentlessly for his client's innocence. If Garrett wanted to talk to her, he would keep returning until she agreed.

"If not for me," he added. "For Callie."

Guilt coated Taryn's mouth like icky-tasting cold medicine. She hadn't considered her friend, who was already stressed about the upcoming wedding. Callie didn't need anyone else adding to that.

Taryn swiveled in her chair to face him. "Talk."

"I owe you an apology." His voice was gruff, and Garrett cleared his throat. "I said I'd call, but I received death

49

threats."

Six months after ghosting her, this was what he'd come up with. She scoffed. "Sure you did."

His nostrils flared. "Why would I lie?"

She shrugged. "I'm guessing Callie asked you to talk to me. Death threats sound like a convenient, albeit out-there excuse, even for a lawyer from L.A."

Garrett blew out a breath. He removed his cell phone from his pocket, tapped on the screen, and held the phone toward her.

A sharp, loud sound made her cringe. Two more quickly followed.

"What's that?" she asked.

"Gunshots left on my voicemail the day I returned from Silver Falls. A creepy letter arrived at my office the next day. That evening, I came home to a message on my bathroom mirror written in blood. Someone slipped past the doorman and lobby security and broke into my condo." His nostrils flared again. "Not an excuse."

"I…" She didn't know what to say. "This kind of stuff happens on TV."

"And in real life. At least in mine." He didn't miss a beat. "I went dark. That was the only way to keep myself and those close to me safe until the police found who threatened me."

That was the last thing Taryn expected to hear. "Thanks for thinking of my safety."

"I should have told you what was going on."

She would give him the benefit of the doubt. "You had

other things on your mind. It must have been scary."

"It was difficult." His words came out slow as if he had to force each one. He hadn't spoken like that in December. "I wouldn't call threats an occupational hazard as a trial attorney, but this guy didn't threaten only me. I didn't want anyone…hurt because of me."

"Especially your family."

He nodded once.

"Is everything okay now?" she asked.

"The police arrested him. He was sloppy. Left so many trails of evidence it made the case a slam dunk. But once everything was resolved, so much time had passed. It would have been strange, awkward, to call you then. I'm sorry."

His apology sounded sincere, and the situation must have been frightening. At least he was safe. His family, too. Though she might have erased the message with the gunshots, not carry it around like evidence or a badge of honor.

Still, holding a grudge made no sense. Other than at Callie and Brandt's wedding, they wouldn't see each other. "Apology accepted."

"Thank you." Garrett rubbed his neck. "I never meant to lead you on. I thought we agreed about not being interested in a relationship. I'm sorry if I gave you the wrong idea about us."

*Oh, no.* Taryn needed this to stop before it went any further. "I agreed with you and feel the same as I did then, but I didn't appreciate being ghosted with what's been going on in my life. I wasn't in love with you or heartbroken. We had fun, but we barely knew each other. I was upset over being dismissed so easily."

"Oh." Garrett shifted his weight between his feet.

Her mouth was so dry it was as if she'd forgotten to add eggs to a cake mixture. "Anything else?"

His features relaxed. So did his posture. "No."

"Enjoy dessert with your family."

He opened his mouth before closing it.

"What?" she asked.

"Nothing." He rocked back on his heels. "I'll see you around."

Not if Taryn could help it.

# Chapter Five

THE NEXT DAY, Garrett typed an email to his assistant, Teresa. The name reminded him of Taryn. Okay, only three letters were the same, but it was close enough. He'd only left Margot's house to take the dogs on a walk, but he'd gone in the opposite direction of First Avenue to avoid the bakery. But that didn't stop him from thinking about Taryn.

He rubbed the back of his neck to ease the tension building in the cords.

His mind kept piecing together snippets of conversations he'd had with Taryn and Jayden. Like a jigsaw puzzle, the pieces fit well.

But he didn't like the picture forming—Taryn and the bakery were in trouble.

Financial? Legal? Health?

Callie had mentioned a bakery in Summit Ridge. Was that it?

His stomach hardened.

It shouldn't matter. Taryn's problem wasn't his. She'd made her feelings clear. They'd had fun in December, but there wasn't more there. He'd told himself the same thing in January and again in April, using it as an excuse for not contacting her.

In theory, the argument worked.

In reality?

Her words bristled more than they should. She wasn't a girlfriend or an ex, but someone he'd hung out with for two weeks.

*Focus, Andrews.*

Garrett tapped on his laptop, the clicking of keys providing background noise in the quiet house. Margot was at her quilt shop. She'd taken the dogs with her so they could spend some time with Callie at the doggy daycare. He should make the most of the quiet.

But random thoughts of Taryn distracted him.

Garrett read over the email, attached his notes, and hit *send.* He glanced at the clock.

Eleven.

The rest of the day was free now.

A door slammed.

Given the way Callie and Brandt came in and out of Margot's house as if it were their own, it could be any of the three. Garrett hoped it was his sister so he could ask her what she needed him to do.

He went downstairs.

In the entryway, Margot dug through her tote. Her long, gauzy skirt swayed with her movements. "Working hard?"

"I was."

She pulled something out of her bag, smiled as if she'd found the Holy Grail, and held up her cell phone. "I knew it had to be in there."

He tapped his back pocket. His phone was there. "Glad you found it."

"Me, too." She typed on the phone. "What are you doing today?"

"I finished what I needed to do for today. Do you need me to run errands?"

She glanced up. "I need your taste buds."

He hadn't expected to hear that. "How so?"

"I need another opinion on what the rehearsal dessert bar should include. Otherwise, it'll be my favorites."

"Count me in." His stomach growled in agreement. "I'm an expert on sweet treats. I'm happy to share my thoughts. Where's your list?"

"No list. We're doing a tasting."

His mouth went dry. He scratched the top of his hand, almost not wanting to ask, but he needed to know. "Where?"

"At the bakery."

Of course, there. Where else would Margot buy desserts in Silver Falls?

Okay, he and Taryn were adults. This was business. Still, the itchiness continued, and a warning sounded in his head. "As long as we're only there to taste sweets and not have you play matchmaker."

"Moi?" She motioned to herself. "You asked me not to interfere during this visit."

Which implied she would the next time Garrett came to town. No worries. He would deal with that when it happened. Not that he wanted to change his mind after agreeing, but Margot was the center of the town's gossip circle. He didn't need her getting suspicious about Taryn and him.

"What time do we leave?" he asked.

"A little before one. We'll pick up the dogs on the way home. I left them with Callie so they could play with their friends longer rather than be here alone."

She spoke as if Angus and Sadie were human, not canines. Given she treated them like children, that shouldn't surprise him.

"I'll fix lunch," Margot added.

"Or I can take you out."

Her face brightened. "A meal with a handsome younger man. I'm in."

Nearly two hours later, at the Falls Café, they'd laughed their way through salads and entrées. They'd skipped dessert because of the tasting.

"Thank you." Margot sat her empty glass of lemonade on the table. "This is the best lunch I've had in a long time."

Garrett signed the receipt. Margot was a twenty-first-century version of *Auntie Mame*. "It was delicious, but the company was better."

"It was." She leaned against her chair with a satisfied expression. "I could get used to this."

He scooted forward. "Why don't you find yourself a match?"

Her cheeks reddened. "No. I couldn't."

"I need more than that."

"This isn't a cross-examination, counselor."

"We're having a friendly conversation." He emphasized

the second to last word.

"Well." She glanced around the café before lowering her voice. "Have you seen the single men in town?"

Leave it to Margot. His grin spread. "No."

"Most of the available ones are widowers of my friends who passed. Lovely women, but I didn't know why they married the men or stayed with them."

He laughed. "You don't have to limit yourself to Silver Falls. There are dating apps."

She shook her head. "I needed Brandt to explain the new remote for my TV. Knowing me, I'd swipe left when I wanted to swipe right and mess up everything." She reached across the table and patted his hand. "That's sweet of you to think of me, but I'll stick to what I'm good at: living alone, quilting, and fixing up other people."

"As long as I'm not one of the other people, I can live with that."

She wagged her finger. "When you see who I have in mind for Keaton, you'll want me to find you someone, too."

"As long as you wait until I ask."

With a harrumph, she stood. "Let's go, so we're not late."

They stepped outside, and a wave of heat hit. The bakery was only a few storefronts away, but sweat dotted his hairline and the back of his neck. He should have worn shorts instead of khakis.

As Garrett opened the bakery door for Margot, the electronic ping brought memories of his last visit to mind. He hoped this one went better. If he were the superstitious type, which he wasn't, he would cross his fingers.

"We're here for the dessert tasting." She waved at Jayden, who stood behind the counter.

A weight lifted from Garrett. Maybe Taryn wasn't here. He didn't think his presence would upset her, or he'd never agree to come, but keeping distance between them until the wedding seemed like a smart idea.

The baker smiled at Margot and ignored Garrett. That was fine by him.

Jayden motioned to the eating area. "Take a seat, and we'll be right with you."

Did "we" include Taryn?

Garrett couldn't see into the kitchen, so he followed Margot to a table. Not that she had to worry about finding one. "The items here are better than any bakery I've visited in L.A. I can't believe it's so empty."

She sat, shaking her head. "It's such a shame. This place has the best desserts around, but blame that no-good Nick Baxter, who convinced investors to open a bakery in Summit Ridge. That's the closest town and has a university."

He took the seat next to her. "Keaton toured the college in December, but the name sounds familiar."

Margot's expression soured. "He's Brandt's former best friend and business partner."

"The one who sold the company out from under him?"

"One and the same."

That must be the issue Jayden meant last night. "The guy sounds slimy."

"He is. He was a sweet boy, but he's nothing like the kid

I used to know." Margot came closer. "Let me tell you, the other is a pale comparison to this one, but they're drawing in customers with the rock-bottom prices and destroying this place."

Taryn must be freaking out. "Can Lawson's hang on?"

"I hope so." Margot's voice didn't have the usual confidence. "The bakery's had no competition until now. Her father believes the newness will blow over."

"I hope he's correct."

"Me, too, but Taryn's doing what she can in the meantime."

Garrett glanced at the back door that wasn't there in December. There'd only been the one in the kitchen, which they'd used to leave by after she closed the bakery. "The patio?"

Margot nodded. "Her competition has only a small eating area, and it's inside, so this sets Lawson's apart. Plus, people enjoy having a new place to go in the evenings."

In the summer and early fall, at least. Once the rain and snow hit, no one would want to sit outside, but he didn't want to be the Debbie Downer.

"I wish Lawson's well." But that was all Garrett should do. This wasn't his problem to fix. He needed to focus on the task at hand. "So, what do I need to know about the dessert tasting?"

"Callie and Brandt don't want cake since they're having that at the wedding."

"Makes sense."

Margot rolled her eyes. "You can never have too much

cake."

"True, but I see why they want a variety."

"I knew you were the right man for this job."

"Flattery will get you everywhere, especially with baked goods involved."

It was Margot's turn to laugh.

Jayden set water glasses on the table before removing papers and pencils from his apron pocket and placing them next to the drinks. "Taryn will be right out. She's running late."

That surprised him. She was always early.

Margot raised her glass. "We're in no rush. I'm relishing every moment of my part of the wedding planning."

"And I'm contributing my taste buds to the effort," Garrett said.

The corners of Jayden's mouth lifted. "It's good to have two opinions."

Did that mean the baker forgave Garrett? He hoped so. "Happy to give mine."

Taryn hurried out. "I'm sorry I'm late."

A teenager with short red hair and freckles carried a tray. He placed the desserts on the table. Each plate had a number on it. "Anything else, Boss?"

"No," she said. "Thanks, Brecken."

"Check the dough, Brecken," Jayden said before turning to Taryn. "Holler, if you need me."

With a nod, Taryn sat, and her right arm hit the table. She winced, cradling her bandaged hand.

None of his business, but Garrett had to ask. "Did you

burn your hand?"

Taryn startled as if surprised he was there. "Uh, no. I had a mishap with a hammer this morning."

"Oh, no." Margot's face scrunched. "The patio's finished. What were you doing with a hammer?"

Taryn blew out a breath. "Working on the bakery's booth for the summer fair."

"I thought you finished it last year," Margot said.

"I did, but when I opened the shed to put it together, I found everything wet and moldy. Water got inside somehow, and I have to start over."

She sounded more resigned than upset, which surprised Garrett. He remembered how spectacular her Christmas window had been in December. He assumed she would have put the same effort into another project.

"It starts on Friday afternoon." Margot rubbed her chin. "Can you finish on time?"

"I've got my work cut out for me, but I'll get it done." Determination laced each of Taryn's words, telling him she would even if it killed her.

"You need help." The sentence flew out of his mouth.

Taryn shrugged. "I'm using the same theme as before, but it took me two weeks working each night to make the first one. Jayden wants me to ask a paramedic for help."

Margot perked up. "Do you mean the new guy with gray eyes, a killer smile, and to-die-for body who asked you out a few months ago, and you turned down?"

"Yes. I said no yesterday when Jayden brought it up." Taryn held up her bandaged hand. "But I'm not sure I have a choice. I'll be upfront about what's going on, so he doesn't get the wrong idea."

"Go for it," Margot encouraged. "Be upfront, but you might still end up with a boyfriend or husband out of the deal."

Taryn blushed.

Margot's matchmaking must extend beyond family members, but Garrett didn't like the idea of Taryn being forced to rely on someone's help if she hadn't wanted to go out with the guy before.

"I need the booth ready on time." Taryn lowered her arm. "If I knew anyone with construction know-how who was free over the next couple of days, I'd ask them. But people are too busy."

Garrett had experience and the time, but he didn't have to speak up. If he said nothing, no one would know.

Not true.

He would.

The cons of offering ran through this mind—his workload, helping with the wedding, how things stood between them, and Taryn falling for the hottie helper, who must be interested in her if he asked her out. Only had one pro appeared—helping her would allow him to make amends for his actions—but that was enough. "If you're flexible about the time of day, I can help."

"You?" she and Margot asked at the same time.

Okay, he usually sat behind a desk in a corner office or stood in front of a courtroom. His hands weren't calloused and scarred, but... "I've worked on Habitat for Humanity projects for over fifteen years. I picked up a few construction skills."

"Wonderful." Margot clapped her hands together. "You'll finish faster with two people working on the booth."

Taryn said nothing, but she dragged her upper teeth over her lower lip.

"I'm happy to help." He wanted her to be as pleased by his offer as Margot was. "If you want my help."

"Of course she wants it." Margot sounded as if this were a done deal. "Isn't that right, dear?"

Taryn swallowed. "I could use a hand, especially now that I hurt mine, but—"

"No buts," Margot interrupted.

Taryn looked at Garrett, but he couldn't read her face. The dark circles under her eyes suggested she wasn't sleeping enough. She might consider him an enemy, but he'd been shouted at, attacked, and threatened by attorneys and clients. If it were for the right reason like making up for what he'd done, he could handle pretty much anything, including a hostile work environment.

"I'm up for it." Whatever "it" entailed. His voice remained confident, even if his insides twisted. "If you are."

She gave a slight nod. If Garrett hadn't been so focused on her, he would have missed it. "Okay."

Her soft, tentative tone made him want to hug her and say it would all work out. But he couldn't. "Okay."

"It's settled." Margot studied the desserts. "Now, tell us about these delicious treats you've prepared for us, and after we've finished, you two can figure out the booth while I get

Angus and Sadie from Callie's."

If Garrett didn't know better, he would think Margot orchestrated this. But not even the Silver Falls matchmaker extraordinaire would have ruined the first booth.

Taryn inhaled, her features relaxing. "Use the paper in front of you to make notes. The numbers on the plate will help you keep track of what's what."

"That's smart." Margot shot him a sideways glance. "Isn't that smart of her, Garrett?"

Maybe Margot hadn't given up on the matchmaking. A pain formed at his temple. He rubbed the spot to stave off a headache. "It is."

What else could he say? Especially now they would work together. But that gave him an idea. He would try to finish the booth in two days. That would be better than three.

"I chose Callie and Brandt's favorites along with a couple of our top sellers. I picked ones that complement each other and appeal to a wide range of tastes." Taryn didn't miss a beat. "Rather than have you try them in any specific order, I'd like you to each pick one to start. You can use the water to cleanse your palate in between bites."

"I'd like to try the miniature pie." Margot peered closer. "Number five."

"That's a mini-marionberry pie. I can make any flavor of pie if you have a favorite."

Margot shimmied her shoulders. "Oh, I love marionberries."

"Marionberries?" he asked.

"They were first grown in Marion County in Oregon but

are becoming popular all over these days," Taryn explained. "I use them when they're in season, which is now, and I keep some frozen or canned during the winter."

"For Mr. Jones's birthday?" Margot asked.

Taryn laughed. "He loves them, and a person should have their favorite dessert on the day of their birth."

Now, this was the woman Garrett remembered. Warmth spread through him. The confident baker never forgot details about her clients and went out of her way for them, even if it meant watching an anime show so she could create a custom cake for a kid's fourteenth birthday. She'd done that in December.

Taryn stared at him.

His heart jolted as if a 7.0 earthquake struck.

*Whoa.* That was unexpected.

"Did you pick the one you wanted to try first?" she asked.

Garrett hadn't because of his attention on her. He swallowed.

"Number three." He picked that one because he assumed if there were a five, the first four numbers would be there, too.

Taryn raised a brow. "I didn't think you liked mousse."

*Busted.* Garrett glanced at the plate. Number three turned out to be a chocolate shell filled with pink mousse. "It looks like something Callie would enjoy."

There. He'd saved himself.

Taryn eyed him suspiciously. "It's one of her favorites at Christmastime. Only since it's July, I replaced the peppermint mousse with raspberry."

"I don't need to taste it." She'd given him an out, and he would take it. "Callie will love it. Especially if you add chocolate shavings and a raspberry on top."

"Oh, perfect additions." Margot picked up her pencil. "I'll write those down. I had no idea you knew so much about desserts, Garrett."

"Me, either." Taryn's laughter-filled gaze, however, told another story.

Did she remember making him a similar dessert at her house? Or that he'd scooped out the mousse and eaten the shavings, raspberry, and chocolate cup, instead?

"It's a gift." One Garrett hoped got him through the next few days of helping Taryn, or his sister's wedding might become an uncomfortable try-to-avoid-each-other event.

# Chapter Six

AFTER MARGOT LEFT to pick up her dogs, Taryn sat with Garrett. His blue polo shirt and khakis made him look more like someone taking a late lunch during his workday than a person on a summer vacation. The way he dressed so well had caught her eye in December. Most guys in town thought dressing up meant showering and wearing after-shave.

Not Garrett.

The only differences between winter and summer were the short sleeves and his hair, something she hadn't noticed yesterday. Ends curled and brushed his collar. The style wasn't as corporate as before. It suited him.

Not that she cared how he dressed or looked now.

But the same care he took with his appearance seeped into everything he did—from inviting her out to dinner the first time or helping decorate her Christmas tree when he realized she hadn't gotten around to it. Did his more carefree style mean that had changed?

"Do you need to know anything else for the dessert buffet?" he asked.

She glanced at the sheets with his and Margot's notes.

"We should be good. Ideas are swirling in my head. Plus, I want to make sure the items won't melt in the backyard."

"I forgot the rehearsal dinner is outside."

"I've done plenty of outdoor events in the heat, and I have a week and a half to figure it out. Now the booth…"

That was another story. Taryn slumped before straightening.

No getting discouraged, or she might as well give up.

He said nothing. Neither did she.

Did that mean he wasn't going to help her?

Taryn needed help, but she didn't want to need his help.

Ugh. She couldn't make sense of anything right now.

Her temperature rose. Taryn fought the urge to fan herself to cool down.

Thick tension hung in the air, intensifying the silence and increasing the distance between them.

Her desperation or his regret? A combination of both?

Taryn needed to find out, but she would give him an out. That was the polite thing to do. "I appreciate you wanting to help, but I know your time is limited. You're on vacation and have wedding stuff to do with Callie."

His jaw tightened. "I wouldn't have offered if I couldn't do it."

"Great. I mean, thank you." She paused for a moment to breathe. "It's…"

So much for knowing what to say. Taryn bit her lip.

"This feels weird after how comfortable things were between us before," he said finally.

She was happy he said it and not her, but at least he felt

it, too.

"It does." When Garrett had first offered, something inside Taryn screamed N-O! Until she remembered her injured hand. That would slow her down when she needed to speed up. "As much as I want to build the booth myself, I can't do this on my own."

That should have been harder for her to admit, but pretending wouldn't make things better. Accepting help—Garrett's help—was the only way to finish on time.

His gaze met hers. "You don't have to."

"I appreciate that." But knowing she wouldn't be all on her own didn't ease her knotted muscles. Her future was at stake. That was another reality she couldn't ignore.

Still, working with Garrett was better than relying on Rachelle's friend, who was more of an unknown quantity beyond his love for apple fritters and macaroons. At least, she hoped that was the case.

Taryn needed to make sure she could count on him or she was calling the paramedic. "I didn't want you to feel obligated just because Margot was here."

"I don't." Amusement flickered in his eyes.

Taryn didn't know what was so funny unless it was her.

She gathered the two pieces of paper notes and pens off the table, nearly snapping off the lid on one pen. "I'll put these away and get the plans for the booth."

"I can't wait to see what you came up with."

The sincerity in his voice had to be a good sign, right? Or he was using the acting skills he'd honed during trials.

No. She should think positive, but after a string of bad

luck, it was difficult, which was why she second-guessed everything, including herself.

"How long did you say it took you to put the booth together the first time?" he asked.

She crinkled the papers in her hand. "Every night for two weeks."

"And we have three days." No judgment sounded in his tone, but lines tightened around his mouth.

His "we" sent warmth flowing through her. "I've brainstormed ways of simplifying the original design. I…we can't redo it the same, or it'll never be ready in time."

"Sounds smart."

"More like a Hail Mary pass."

He laughed. "I forgot you were a big football fan."

She shrugged, not wanting to care he hadn't remembered that when they'd watched games, as in plural, over the holidays. "It will only take us a few minutes to go over the plans."

Garrett stretched out his legs. "I'm in no rush."

Unfortunately, she was. "I won't be long."

Part of the reason she'd hurt her hand was not sleeping last night. If she'd had the materials, Taryn would have worked on the booth. Instead, she'd lain in bed, going over what she needed to do and simplifying the design without affecting the quality too much.

*Thinking won't get it done.*

She hurried into the kitchen. Jayden and Brecken stood at the stainless steel table working. Typical. But the usual chatter was subdued. That happened on Carl's day off. That guy was a regular magpie. Finley would be there to work from six until close so she could stay home tonight.

"How'd the tasting go?" Jayden held a pastry bag full of chocolate buttercream icing.

"Great. Margot and Garrett both loved your brownie bites."

"Score!" He pumped his free fist. "So glad I remembered brownies are Brandt's favorite."

"Yep. I need to grab stuff from the office before I head home."

"Good luck." Jayden winked. "And the hammer."

"Not funny."

Brecken laughed. "Yes, it is, Boss."

"I'll laugh when my hand doesn't hurt." Taryn headed into her office. She glanced at the plans on the bulletin board before picking up the copies she'd made at lunchtime so she'd have a set at home, too.

Clothes were in her locker, but she would change out of whites—Lawson's uniform for the past fifty years—when she got home. That way, Garrett didn't have to wait longer. She removed her hat and hairnet before grabbing her purse.

"The specials are on the board and ready to go outside." That was the only task she'd needed to complete since Carl was off. He had the best handwriting, so he usually wrote that night's menu. "Take care."

"Good luck with the booth." Brecken glanced up from the bread he'd pulled from the oven. "We've got everything under control."

"I know." And why Taryn could turn off her cell phone

if she wanted. "But if you get slammed with customers—"

"Finley will be here later." Jayden shooed her away. "Go build us the winning booth."

"On my way." She adjusted her purse strap before heading out of the kitchen.

As soon as she saw Garrett at the table, her hand tightened around the plans, crinkling the paper. He sat as if being the only non-bakery employee in the place was normal at two o'clock on a Tuesday. At least her parents weren't there to see it.

Taryn swallowed a sigh.

She loosened her grip. "Sorry to keep you waiting."

"It's fine." He glanced at the empty tables. "Slow day?"

A lump burned in her throat, and her breath hitched. *Do. Not. Cry.*

After exhaling, she placed the plans on the table and sat.

"Yes," her voice cracked.

She cringed, but the emptiness of the one thing she loved wholeheartedly pressed all her buttons and not in a good way. No one had stopped in to purchase a loaf of bread or rolls for dinner. No one had popped by for a cookie or a cupcake. No one had ordered a special dessert for a celebration in the upcoming days.

Taryn's stomach churned. She couldn't remember the last time that had happened.

Even with the patio's grand opening this past weekend, business was getting worse. People might visit during evening hours, but that wasn't generating any day traffic.

"Are you okay?" The concern in Garrett's voice matched

the look in his eyes.

Taryn would kill for a hug. Instead, she raised her chin. *You can do this.*

She didn't have a choice unless her father decided otherwise. "Yeah, a lot's going on."

He glanced around. "Margot mentioned a new bakery in Summit Ridge."

"They opened a few months ago. We've taken a big hit." Taryn glanced at the door, willing for someone to enter to show the situation wasn't hopeless, but no one did. "Now the booth is ruined, and it feels like everything is going wrong."

"My showing up didn't help."

No." Heat rushed up to her neck. She squirmed in her seat. "I mean…"

"I know what you mean."

Did he? Because Taryn wasn't sure she did. "I appreciate you offering to help. There's no way I could do this on my own."

"Then let's get this done."

His confidence gave her a much-needed boost.

With a closed-mouth smile, he leaned forward. "Show me your plans."

The plans, right. She pushed the design toward him. "My theme is *A Midsummer Night's Dream*."

Garrett glanced up at her. "From Tchaikovsky at Christmas to Shakespeare in the summer."

Taryn shrugged, but not out of indifference. She took the business association's competitions seriously and had filled a notebook with ideas for themes.

"Lawson's Bakery has never won the booth competition, so I wanted to come up with something extra special. I did this without knowing the other bakery would open this year. The booth resembles the woods outside of Athens. The goal is to make it appear whimsical and magical, using edible decorations."

He paged through the sheets of paper. "You put a lot of thought into this."

"I did. Last fall, I spent every night after work and all day on Sundays working on it. There isn't time to replicate the exact design, but I'd like it to be as close as possible."

"So before we talk about the actual plans, what is the booth for, and where will it be set up?"

Oh, right. This was only Garrett's second time visiting his sister. "The First Avenue Business Association sponsors events throughout the year. The Silver Falls Summer Fair is one of the bigger ones. It starts on Friday afternoon and runs through Sunday in the park. There are booths. Food trucks come in. There are rides and games and entertainment. It's a big draw with visitors from here and nearby towns."

"Sounds fun. So your booth is for the bakery."

She nodded. "Each First Avenue business is given space to showcase their products or services and interact with the public by giving samples or having a giveaway. The association offers a prize for the best booth theme to make sure businesses don't show up with only a table and pop-up tent."

"So this is like the Christmas window contest Callie won."

"Yes. But unlike the Christmas window competition, the public votes for their favorite booth. The winner is announced on Friday evening, so they have bragging rights over the next two days." Taryn wrung her hands before placing them on her lap. "The prize isn't as big as what your sister won in December, but a first-place win gets exposure on the town's website and social media. Winning would get our name out there so we can draw in new customers."

"And bring back old ones."

She straightened, fighting the urge to square her shoulders. This wasn't a battle, even if saving the bakery felt like one. "My focus is on finding new ones."

He opened his mouth before closing it. His eyebrows furrowed. "Will that be hard in a town this size?"

"Yes, especially since we've been in the same location for fifty years. I thought we had a loyal customer base, but I see now they bought here because we were the only bakery nearby. They left for the lower prices in Summit Ridge, not caring the gas money they spend driving there makes the savings a wash." She grimaced at her harsh tone. But her dad blamed her for the losses, not the competition, even though they'd had their best year ever before the other bakery opened. "Sorry if I sound bitter. But to be honest, I am bitter."

"Understandable." He tilted his head, his gaze never leaving hers. "You also sound tired."

"I am."

"There's nothing wrong with wanting loyal customers. That's how businesses thrive." Garrett leaned forward, nearly pressing against the table's edge. "The design looks cool but complicated."

"There are many pieces, but the yellow highlighted lines are the simplified version."

"The original looked more like a frame with tree-trunk sides."

"Yes, I wanted it to be like a painting with a display of samples in the center." She pointed to a drawing. "The trees are staying, but tulle, garland, fairy lights, and a sign hanging off the pop-up tent's frame will replace the top portion. It's simpler but should give the same effect. We'll add the final layer of decorations, which are baked goods that resemble flowers, animals, and birds, to those. But that won't happen until the booth is at the park."

"How much have you redone?"

Her knee bounced. She pressed her unbandaged hand against it. "I ordered the supplies yesterday and picked them up from the hardware store this morning. I was working on the front piece when the hammer met my hand up close and personal."

He grinned wryly. "Hate when that happens."

"Me, too."

Her gaze collided with his, only this time something passed between them. Not tension. Almost a current of some sort. Attraction.

Nope. No way.

Lesson learned. She would not go that route with Garrett again.

His help and good looks wouldn't sway her.

She swallowed before refocusing on the plans. "Things will make more sense when you see the actual pieces."

He looked over each of the pages again. "When do you want to start?"

"I'm going home now to work on it. Jayden and my staff are covering for me the next few days until it's finished."

Garrett glanced at his phone. "Callie's hosting a family dinner tonight, but I'm free for a couple of hours this afternoon."

"That's fine. Great." The words flew out of Taryn's mouth. "I mean, there's no set schedule, and you're doing me a favor. Stop by when you have time. If you don't have as much as you originally thought, no worries. You're in town to help your sister with the wedding, not build a booth."

*Oh, no.* She was rambling.

"I want to help, Taryn. And I will."

Tears welled behind her eyelids. She blinked them away.

"But Callie is my priority," he added.

The words pierced Taryn's heart with bull's-eye precision. Someday, she wanted to be someone's priority. "I know. And that's how it should be."

"But I'll do as much as I can between now and Friday."

"I appreciate it."

As she stacked the pages, her hand bumped against his. Tingles shot up her arm. Taryn needed to avoid him as she did the hammer. "I'll give you my address."

His eyebrow creased. "I remember where you live."

*Oh, right.* He hadn't forgotten. "See you there."

"It won't take me long. I need to run to Margot's and

change into shorts and a T-shirt."

Taryn nodded.

"This doesn't have to be so awkward." He brushed his hand through his hair. "I'm a friend helping another friend."

She'd never thought of him that way, but if it made things more comfortable when they were together, she would give "friends" a try. "That'll work."

"If it doesn't, I have a feeling we'll be so busy we don't notice," he teased.

His grin brightened his face, showing off sun-kissed skin that intensified the color of his eyes. So handsome.

Her heart kicked up a notch.

*Uh-oh.* Taryn's breath caught. Maybe she should have asked Rachelle's paramedic friend for help instead.

# Chapter Seven

AN HOUR LATER, Garrett stood on Taryn's porch, his finger hovering in front of the doorbell. The welcome sign hanging on the door mocked him. The hair on his neck lifted as if agreeing that he shouldn't be there.

He wanted to make up for what he'd done, but he'd forgotten sometimes that wasn't possible. He was older and wiser than he'd been as a summer intern, but would his wanting to help Taryn turn out the same way that experience had?

Garrett hoped not, but doubts grew, swamping his desire to make amends, and he lowered his hand. Except...

Taryn had appeared to be on the verge of tears at the bakery.

Walking away wasn't an option.

Not after saying he'd help and knowing she needed something to go right when everything else had gone wrong. Whether or not he proved himself was no longer the point. This was about Taryn.

Sure, the image of being a knight in shining armor out to rescue her appealed to him at a gut level. Who didn't want to be someone's hero? But his armor was tarnished in her eyes.

Besides, Taryn Lawson was more than capable of rescuing herself. She just needed a hand—any hand—and his was, well, handy.

Time to stop with the theatrics, even if they were only in his mind. He wasn't being paid to stand in front of a jury, who would rather be at the grocery store or sitting in a dental chair having their teeth cleaned than in a courtroom. He was there to help someone in need.

*You're all she's got.*

At least based on what he'd heard from Margot when he'd asked if she knew others who might be able to help with Taryn's booth this week.

His cell phone buzzed. His sister's name showed on the screen. Perfect timing. Garrett had asked if she knew anyone, too.

**Lil' Sis:** *I called a few people to see if anyone else can help Taryn, but no luck.*

**Lil' Sis:** *Rumor has it Mr. Jones from the hardware store is so behind he's dropping out.*

**Lil' Sis:** *So you're it for Taryn.*

**Lil' Sis:** *For help, I mean.*

**Lil' Sis:** *Please don't hurt her again.*

Okay, he was the only help Taryn would have. But the last line bristled. He reread it.

Why would he hurt Taryn?

The cold temperatures, snow, and wreath on the door were long gone. He wiped the sweat from his forehead with the back of his hand. Memories of eating dinner, watching holiday movies, drinking eggnog, and kissing—no mistletoe required—would fade, as would ones they created with their newly minted friendship.

*Friends.*

That would appease his sister. He typed.

**Garrett:** *Thanks for seeing if anyone else could help.*

**Garrett:** *I can't hurt her.*

**Garrett:** *Taryn and I are just friends.*

Friends who had some explosive chemistry based on when they'd accidentally touched at the bakery, but "friends" didn't think about past or present kisses. There was no chance for future ones, so those weren't an issue.

**Lil' Sis:** *Glad to hear it.*

**Lil' Sis:** *I just want to make sure you wouldn't screw anything up for the wedding.*

**Garrett:** *I'll be on my best behavior. Promise.*

And he would. Garrett only pushed the rules when he knew he could get away with it. He didn't want to upset Callie or Taryn. Especially her.

Not again.

The truth was, he wished the Taryn he remembered from December would return. That woman had been all sunshine and smiles. It was time to bring out her dimples.

With a goal in mind, Garrett pressed the doorbell.

A chime announced his arrival, and the door opened less than a minute later.

"Hello." Taryn had changed out of her white baker's

outfit and into a pair of blue shorts and a green T-shirt with paint stains.

He stared at her legs.

Why hadn't he noticed them before?

They went on forever. Okay, he'd been here in winter when it was snowing, but she should move to a warmer climate so she could show them off year-round.

"Garrett?"

*Oops.* A friend probably shouldn't stare at another friend's legs.

His gaze jerked to her pretty face. No dimples or grin, but those would come. That was why he was here. Couldn't forget that.

"I'm here. Ready to get started." He fought the urge to cringe. So much for being an eloquent orator.

Her gaze ran the length of him. Her expression pinched. "You're not wearing grubbies."

She wasn't wrong. His wardrobe came from a high-end department store where a personal shopper selected outfits for him. "This is as casual as I packed."

She motioned him inside. "I'll paint, so you don't stain your clothes."

He stepped into the house, cold air surrounding him. Her sugary scent held a touch of lemon now. He didn't know what refreshed him more—the temperature or the way she smelled.

"Everything's set up in the backyard." Taryn headed toward the kitchen. "We can work on the patio. It's covered and will be cooler in the shade."

Garrett forced himself not to stare at her legs. A friend could look, but leering would be creepy. He glanced around her house instead.

An overstuffed chair and ottoman were where the Christmas tree had been. Food magazines and cookbooks sat on the coffee table. Otherwise, it was the same as he remembered from his last visit.

He stepped into the kitchen. On the table were shopping bags with garlands and other items. Decorations for the booth?

Taryn grabbed two bottles of water from the fridge and handed one to him. "Stay hydrated. Margot and Callie will never forgive me if you suffer heat exhaustion."

The bottle cooled his palm. "I live in Southern California. I'm used to hot weather."

"But how often do you work outside?"

She had a point. He unscrewed the lid and took a sip. "Might as well cool off from my walk over here."

"There are more water bottles in here. Help yourself when you need another."

When not if. That brought a smile. He hadn't noticed Taryn's caretaker side before, but a nurturer who also baked and kissed like a dream was a perfect combination. Well, if he was in the market for either of those things. Which he wasn't.

He drank more. "You've thought of everything."

"I try." Taryn opened the sliding door, letting in a wall of heat. "Mr. Jones pre-cut the wood I ordered, but I set up the saw in case we need to make adjustments. Each section of the design has a pile with all its parts, so nothing gets lost."

"Good idea to be organized." Garrett stepped outside.

His mouth fell open. This wasn't organized. She'd made mini production lines with tarps beneath each of her "piles." He thought he was good at planning, but Taryn took it to the next level.

She closed the door.

"You've been busy." That was putting it mildly. She'd assembled the square pop-up tent. Two rectangular tables sat underneath. He scratched his head. "When do you sleep?"

"I'm usually up before the sun, even on my days off, so I don't throw off my body clock." She walked to a large sheet of plywood cut in half and painted forest green. A paper with the design lay next to it, along with a hammer and nails. "This piece needs three supports added. It goes against the front of the table, but I like to make sure the pieces are solid and won't fall."

He picked up the paper and scanned the instructions. The supports were triangular-shaped and made from two-by-fours. Sandbags would sit inside them. "The weight keeps it steady."

"They shouldn't fall forward, which would be a problem with kids and pets running around. Sometimes the wind kicks up when you least expect it. We can't be too careful."

Taryn would be a wonderful mom.

*Whoa.* Garrett took a step away from her. Where had that come from?

She stared at the supplies at his feet as if mentally cataloging the items in case she forgot something.

"I'm sure everything is there." He couldn't imagine anything missing, given how organized she was.

"If not, or if you need me to hold the plywood, let me know." She spoke fast, suggesting she was nervous, but he didn't want to make her feel self-conscious or uncomfortable.

"Will do." Garrett expected Taryn to walk away to whatever she'd be working on, but she didn't. He waved the sheet of paper. "I've got this. If I need help, I'll ask."

"Do you need gloves?"

"Not for this." If Garrett needed any, he would buy a pair at the hardware store on the way to his sister's tonight. Speaking of which, he set his phone alarm so he wouldn't be late for dinner.

Taryn picked up a piece of wire fencing. He had no idea what she would do with that or the two pool noodles on top of the tarp, but he wanted to find out.

As she made a cylinder, her tongue stuck out between her lips.

She was a portrait in concentration—a cute one. Which had nothing to do with what she was working on.

Taryn glanced his way, catching his eye. "Have a question?"

"Nope." If Garrett said more, he would incriminate himself. One support was halfway finished. Was that what led to the hammer mishap? He would start with it.

Garrett had built nothing since last summer, but he quickly found his rhythm. He took water breaks and wiped the sweat from his forehead, which was worse from his walk over, but soon he had the three supports constructed and attached to the board.

He stood before pressing against it. "This seems sturdy, even without the sandbags."

"See what happens when you push the other way."

He did, and the piece fell forward and thudded against the tarp. That would hurt if it hit someone. "The supports are an excellent idea. Where do you want this?"

"In front of the table, so we'll get a feel for how this will look."

As he carried the panel to the pop-up tent, a pssst sound caught his attention.

Taryn sprayed the first wire cylinder with plastic sealant. Long strips of foam came out.

He tried to picture what she was making with it—tried and failed.

"It might appear to be globs." She added more between the others. "But it'll look like a tree trunk when I'm finished."

"I didn't know you were a mind reader."

"I'm not, but you looked the way I felt the first time I tried this, but thankfully the instructions I downloaded worked. No Pinterest fail with this."

Garrett had to ask. "Your wording suggests you've suffered at least one fail in the past?"

"Maybe." Her tone was playful. Taryn didn't smile, but she wasn't frowning.

That was a start. "I'll take that as a yes."

She shot a sideward glance his way. "I didn't realize attorneys have such active imaginations."

"Many bestselling authors started as lawyers." He tapped his chin with his finger. "You've got me curious now. Was your fail baking-related?"

She gasped before side-eyeing him. "Are you kidding me?"

He chuckled at her indignation. "I'll take that as a no. So what was it?"

Taryn hesitated. Two lines formed above her nose. "Why do you want to know?"

"To prove you're human and not a robot who does everything from baking to decorating perfectly."

She laughed, a melodic sound he'd forgotten about but which brought back a memory of them making snow angels in this backyard. They'd shared some good times over the holidays.

"I wish, but I'm far from perfect." She sprayed more lines of sealant. "If you don't believe me, ask my dad."

Garrett had never met her father, but if the man had Taryn doubting herself, he didn't want to. "You still haven't told me your fail."

She lowered the can. "I wanted to make a string balloon art for the bakery's front window. The result didn't come close to resembling the photo in the instructions. Imagine the ugliest, abstract pieces of stiff string and multiply them by a thousand. We're talking an epic fail."

"That bad?"

"I still have nightmares about how it turned out."

"Got pics?"

She shook her head. "I deleted them."

That didn't surprise him. Taryn threw her entire self into every project, whether for the bakery, a friend, or even a stranger. "You don't like to fail."

"Does anyone?"

"No, but we learn from our mistakes." Garrett had.

"I learned plenty." She held up her hand and counted off on her fingers. "Never trust an image. Double-check the instructions. Make a prototype first. String art is overrated."

He laughed. "I take it you never tried again."

"Nope. I ended up not decorating, and no one noticed."

His alarm beeped. He shut it off. "The time went fast."

Taryn shrugged. "You know what they say about having fun."

"This has been fun." He glanced at his phone in case he had more time. "I wish I could stay and do more."

"You need to be at Callie's with your family."

He did. They were discussing the wedding and assigning jobs. Since he was here, he would have some say. Flynn and Keaton would be told what to do, having no input. Still, Garrett hated leaving Taryn on her own. "How late will you work tonight?"

"However long it takes." If Taryn wanted to sound lighthearted, she failed. Not only her tone, but the lines on her forehead. "Not all night."

He wasn't sure he believed her. If he returned, that might not happen. The patio had a light. Perhaps that would illuminate the area enough tonight. "I'll stop by after dinner and see if you're still at it."

"I'd appreciate that." She motioned to the side of the

house. "Don't ring the doorbell. I won't hear it if I'm out here. Come through the gate."

He could do that. "What's the keycode or combination?"

"It's open."

"You should have a lock at the minimum. Some type of security device or anyone can enter your backyard without permission."

She laughed. "Silver Falls is nothing like the big city."

No place was immune to troublemakers. "Even small towns have crime. Drug issues. Thefts."

"This place has had all three and more, but I'm safe here."

Her confidence might backfire someday, but he wasn't her keeper. Still… "Please tell me you lock your front door."

"I do, and my slider, too."

That was a relief. "Callie and Margot have locks on their side gates."

"They have dogs." Taryn's matter-of-fact tone didn't loosen the tightness across his chest.

He wanted her to be safe. "It could be for other reasons, too."

"Look up the crime rate in Silver Falls. You'll be surprised."

Been there, done that. "I did when Callie moved here."

"She mentioned her brothers were overprotective."

"We love her and want her to be safe." Garrett also had a detective friend check out the police department to ensure nothing hinky was going on, but only his brothers knew that. "I still recommend locking the doors and securing the gate. You might install cameras and automatic lights."

"If a crime spree hits Silver Falls, I'll consider it." Taryn checked the foam she'd sprayed. "You should take off before you're late."

He should. His family was expecting him. Yet his feet remained planted as if glued to the patio.

"Go," she encouraged. "You've saved my hand from the hammer. Enjoy your dinner and have fun."

"I'll see you soon." Garrett meant it, even if he had to sneak out of Callie's before she served dessert. He had a feeling Taryn would have sweets around here. And returning sooner rather than later might earn him points with her. For what, he didn't know.

But it couldn't hurt.

# Chapter Eight

WEDNESDAY, TARYN WOKE to see nothing but darkness outside her window. Not unusual, but she hadn't expected to start the day as if she were a light and airy fresh-from-the-oven croissant. She should be more tired after working past midnight with Garrett, but the progress they'd made took some pressure off her.

She stretched her arms over her head and pointed her toes.

If they completed as much work today, they would finish the booth on time. Perhaps even early.

A thrill shot through her with a chaser of relief.

Not only about the fair, but about Garrett. Were things comfy and cozy between them, like at Christmastime? Nope, but the awkwardness wasn't as bad as it had been at the bakery. Sure, tension remained, but that hadn't stopped him from working hard. She needed to thank him for his help.

Without him returning after his dinner, she would have pulled an all-nighter. He was making her life so much easier. Not to mention giving her something tasty to look at on her breaks.

Just friends.

But her new friend was gorgeous and, as a baker, it was her occupational duty to investigate delicious things. Or person, in this instance.

She climbed out of bed, grabbed panties, a sports bra, her oldest pair of shorts, and another stained T-shirt. Today, she would paint more, so there was no reason to wear anything nicer.

*Wasn't Garrett reason enough?*

She ignored the little voice in her head. Friends didn't dress up for each other when they were building stuff. And if they weren't working, he wouldn't be here.

End of story.

In the kitchen, she turned on the coffeepot and made a coffee cake.

*For Garrett?*

That voice wouldn't leave her alone. "Yes, it's for him."

The least Taryn could do was feed him while he worked. That was the polite thing to do. Plus, she needed to eat, too.

As the scent of freshly brewed coffee filled the air, she placed the pan in the oven and set the timer. Garrett had a call with his office at eight o'clock and would be over after that. In the meantime, she would have breakfast ready and paint until he arrived.

*It almost sounds like a date.*

No, it didn't.

A meal between friends, that was all.

*Friends.*

She had friends she'd known her entire life, growing up in Silver Falls. She'd also made friends with the new-to-town

First Avenue business shop owners, including Raine Hanover from Tea Leaves and Coffee Beans and Callie Andrews and her groomer, Anna Kent, at Wags and Tails. But none had ever gone out of their way for her like Garrett had. A friend had also never stared at her as much as he did. Not that she hadn't snuck a few peeks at him.

And now, as his friend, she needed to make sure he ate.

After a quick cup of coffee, Taryn headed outside. It was still dark, but the patio light allowed her to see. Her first task involved painting the two cylinders covered in dried foam to give a tree-like appearance. With a brush in hand, she grabbed a can of brown paint, a shade lighter than what she'd used last night. By the time she finished, fingers of purple, orange, and pink rose from the horizon, spreading out across the dawning sky.

Taryn rinsed off the paintbrush and placed it in a bucket. She stood in front of the part Garrett worked on yesterday. He'd not only added the supports but also drilled holes for the miniature white lights. With a stick of chalk, she drew outlines of leaves to paint in a lighter shade of green later.

As the sun cleared the horizon, birds sang.

Their song brought a smile and a rush of gratitude. Despite the competition from Summit Ridge, she had plenty to be thankful for.

She stared at the sky, full of hope. "It's going to be a beautiful day."

"It already is."

Garrett's voice startled her. She glanced over her shoulder.

He wore shorts and a T-shirt. Both were nice enough to be from a designer's collection. Whisker stubble covered his face. The scruff gave him an edgier look. She shouldn't find him so attractive, but…

Her heart thudded.

No, it bumped.

A little one.

Nothing major.

*Friend. Friend. Friend.*

With the mantra looping through her mind, she forced a smile. "Good morning."

He came closer, moving with the grace of an athlete. Not that she was watching him that closely. She swallowed.

He studied the board. "You've accomplished a lot already."

Taryn shrugged. "I'm trying to keep from having another late night."

"Smart plan."

She nodded, but something bugged her. She glanced at the time on her phone. "Didn't you have a call?"

"It was postponed." Garrett wouldn't meet her gaze.

"Did you cancel?"

"I pushed it off, so I could help you."

Her heart melted. Or perhaps appreciation for him gave her the warm fuzzies. "Thank you, but after last night, we're ahead of schedule."

"I want us to stay that way."

Not trusting her voice, she nodded.

"If something important pops up, I'll deal with it, but

this wasn't anything that couldn't wait." He walked to the trees she'd painted. "Now, I see what you meant."

"I'll be nice and not say I told you so," she teased. "I made a coffee cake if you're hungry."

He grinned. "Excellent because I haven't had breakfast."

"There's coffee in the pot, too. Give me a minute."

"Keep drawing." He headed to the house. "I can get it myself. Need anything?"

"Not right now." The way he fit right in, making himself at home, should be weirder. It might be if they hadn't spent those two weeks hanging out here in December. They'd held hands and kissed, but they hadn't labeled themselves as friends or anything else.

But she preferred friends. That was…safer.

And she needed that.

Taryn returned to drawing leaves. After she finished the last one, she grabbed the can of light green paint and a smaller brush. Soon the leaves and vines took shape against the darker forest color.

A sharp sound split the silence.

Hammer against a nail.

She glanced over.

Garrett was adding two-by-ones to construct a frame around the sign. Sweat gleamed on his skin, and his face was flushed.

Staring, she lowered her paintbrush. "Did you eat?"

He nodded. "Loved the coffee cake. I'll want another slice later. You were so focused on painting I didn't want to disturb you."

Taryn hadn't heard him. "How did you know what to do next?"

"Your list. The frame was the next thing."

Her heart swelled with gratitude. "Thanks."

"Things are still in pieces, but once it's all put together, the booth will look great."

"It will." It wouldn't be precisely the same as the original, but that was okay now that she'd gotten over herself. They were doing the best they could under the circumstances, which was all they could do.

He wiped his forehead with his arm. "It's getting hotter."

No kidding. The guy was smokin'.

Would his whiskers scratch her fingertips or cheek?

Not that she would ever find out. "It's almost lunchtime. Let's have a sandwich and cool off inside."

He brushed his hands against his shorts. "Second best offer I've had all day."

"What was the first?"

"The coffee cake."

With a grin, Taryn rinsed off her paintbrush and headed into the house. The cool air surrounded her.

A quick wash of her hands, while Garrett used the hall bathroom, and she prepared sandwiches and filled large glasses with ice cubes and tea.

As they ate, neither spoke, but the silence wasn't uncomfortable.

She placed cookies on a small plate. "Here's dessert."

He took one and bit into it. "So good. Thanks to you, Margot, and Callie, I'll have to hit the gym every day when I get home."

"You're burning off the calories working in the heat."

Garrett winked before taking another cookie. "Then I need more."

"That was easy."

"It's not a hard choice."

He had a point. She took one. "Not bad."

His eyebrows creased. "Didn't you make them?"

"No idea," she admitted. "They're leftovers from the bakery. Employees take home goodie bags when stuff doesn't sell."

"Quite the perk." He finished the second cookie. "Do you get two bags as the owner?"

"One like everyone else. My dad owns the bakery. I'm just an employee."

Garrett studied her with an intense gaze. "Not just. You run the place."

"For now." She bit into her cookie.

Lines formed on his forehead. He leaned forward. "You never mentioned this before. What do you mean for now?"

*Oops.* Taryn hadn't meant to say that. Nor did she want to discuss it. She wiped her mouth with a napkin.

"Taryn?" His voice sharpened.

The bakery's ownership wasn't a secret in town. But Taryn hadn't told anyone, including Jayden, everything because she didn't want to jinx herself and the bakery. Superstitious, maybe? She would rather be safe than sorry with so much at stake, but a part of her wanted to tell someone to keep it from bottling up inside her. Garrett wasn't from around here. Plus, he was an attorney. Weren't they good at keeping secrets?

Better find out.

"Between us?" she asked.

He nodded, coming even closer to her.

Her pulse sped up. But that was likely the situation, not him. At least she hoped so.

Taryn took a breath.

"My dad was thirty when his father signed over the bakery to him. He'd only managed it for a year. I'm thirty-two, and I've run ours without him for three years."

"Why is he waiting?"

A bead of moisture dripped down her glass. She wiped it away with her fingertip. "He doesn't believe I'm capable of running the bakery on my own. Even though he's not there every day, he reviews the books and what I'm doing."

Garrett's lips pressed together. "You were doing fine in December. Has he told you why he feels this way?"

"Not really. Once I took over, profits increased each month until the Summit Ridge Bakery opened in March. At first, he said I wasn't ready to be fully in charge, which I accepted. Now, he's implied I'm not capable."

"Making a profit says you are."

The fact Garrett agreed with her made her sit taller. "I thought so, too, but there must be more to it than that. If I knew what, I could address or fix it."

"His reason might have nothing to do with you."

"I wish I believed that was the case." Snippets from her conversations with her dad swirled in her brain with the force of a hurricane. She shuddered, wanting to shake those words off. "He hates the changes I've made, which is strange because he did the same thing after he took over from his dad. He put his own touch on Lawson's, which is all I want to do, too. At its core, the bakery is the same as it's been for the past fifty years, but I have remodeling plans and more menu ideas to implement. But now…"

"What?"

"He's threatened to sell the bakery."

Garrett's eyes darkened before he sipped his iced tea. "Do you think your dad will?"

She shrugged. "I've been hoping he was joking or trying to stop me making changes, but before he left on his cruise, he said the Summit Ridge people might be better suited to run Lawson's than me."

Garrett's lips parted. "What did you say?"

"Honestly?" Taryn half laughed, but that was only to hide the ache in her heart. "I was too stunned to reply. But what could I say? The bakery belongs to him. He's free to do what he wants with it."

"Yet, you're killing yourself to create a winning booth for this weekend's fair and must have spent hours building the new patio." He rubbed his chin. "Why?"

"That's part of running a business. I know I can make the bakery more profitable. But my dad hates the patio. He called it an enormous waste of time and money and scheduled a cruise to fall during the grand opening. But it's the only thing bringing in sales right now. I hope to use the patio and winning the booth competition to turn things around before my parents get home. All I've ever wanted was to run Lawson's Bakery, and I've worked my entire life to do that. I'm not giving up."

"Don't. Is there anything I can do?" His tone was warm and caring.

Flutters erupted in her stomach. "You're doing plenty by helping with the booth, but thanks for asking."

"Happy to help." Garrett reached toward her before he pulled back his hand. "You're the queen of organization and planning, but do you know what you'll do if he sells the bakery?"

"I only know how to bake and run a bakery." Saying the words left her feeling hollowed out, but she forced herself not to slouch. "I guess I'd try to get a job with whoever bought Lawson's."

"You'd want to do that?"

Her stomach tightened. "It makes the most sense, but the reality might be harder to live with."

"Try impossible."

He was probably right.

She drank, hoping to wash the dryness from her throat. "The other option is to start my own bakery, but a town the size of Silver Falls couldn't support two with a third one a short drive away. I've prayed each night it won't come to that."

He stared over the lip of his glass, keeping the eye contact steady. "I hope it doesn't."

"I'm trying to stay positive about it and don't want to spoil the fun today. At least I've had fun."

"Me, too. We should get back out there." He pushed away from the table. "Finishing isn't only about winning the competition. This is for you, too. So you can show your dad he's wrong."

Joy and gratitude overflowed. He got it. Sure, she had Jayden, but that was at work. Here, now, she didn't feel so all alone. Maybe with Garrett's help, her run of bad luck was about to change.

She crossed her fingers. "T-thank you."

# Chapter Nine

THE AFTERNOON SUN beat down. Garrett had drunk half a case of water today. Possibly more. A shower sounded like heaven, but he wasn't leaving Taryn's backyard. As he sat on a tarp, he held a box cutter in one hand and a pool noodle in the other.

"Looking good." The front panel could easily be used on stage during *A Midsummer Night's Dream*, but he also meant her.

"Thanks." Taryn's face was flushed. Her skin glowed from a layer of sweat. A streak of green paint was on her right cheek, and there were streaks on her hands and T-shirt, too.

He'd never seen her look more beautiful. But it was more than physical.

She pushed sweat-damp strands of hair off her face. "I'm almost finished."

"Me, too."

Taryn had impressed him in December with her dedication to the bakery. He'd assumed she was the owner. Not that he'd asked. But she hadn't blown off her responsibilities to spend time with him, even if that would have made seeing her easier. But his respect shot even higher today, after learning what she'd been going through with her father and not giving up. If anything, she worked harder. The man had to be blind not to realize his daughter's work ethic and loyalty to the bakery and him.

Garrett couldn't imagine many kids—no matter what age—putting up with that kind of treatment from their fathers. He'd been there himself and hadn't returned to his father's law firm for another summer internship. That, however, was in his past. The situation with the bakery was Taryn's present and future.

"There's not much left to do," he said. "What if we grab dinner while the pieces dry?"

"As long as I can shower first." She held up her hands, palms facing him. "I have paint on my paint spots."

"I could use one, too." He tried to remember the restaurants in town. "Margot likes the Fall Café."

"I like that place, but I'm in the mood for pizza."

That wasn't what he expected her to say, but if that was what she wanted, he would buy her pizza. "A pizza parlor or Italian restaurant?"

"There's a place on Main Street called Luigi's. It's my favorite."

"Are reservations required?"

Her grin brightened her face. "Only if you're a baseball, softball, or soccer team. Luigi's is your typical family pizza parlor with sticky tables you wipe yourself and pinball machines older than we are. But the food is to die for."

"Got it. No reservations needed."

She nodded. "If we hadn't been outside all day, I'd suggest taking the food to the park for a picnic, but I'm ready for air-conditioning."

"Me, too." That gave Garrett an idea. "How about we save the picnic for another...time?" He'd almost said date but caught himself.

"Oh, yes. We should do that. I love picnics."

"That's how we'll celebrate finishing the booth."

"Perfect." Her eyes twinkled. "I have a basket and a red-and-white-checked blanket."

"I'm not surprised."

Taryn held up her brush. "The setting is as important as the food."

"I'll have to remember that."

She started to say something before studying the board. "I have a few touch-ups to go."

He sliced the length of the green pool noodle so it would fit around the tent's legs. "This is done, so I'll head to Margot's. Meet you at Luigi's in a half hour."

"Whoever gets there first can grab a table. And so we don't get into an argument there, this is my treat."

He stiffened. "Dinner was my idea."

"You're helping me with the booth, so that's that." She returned to painting.

His entire body seemed to smile. Taryn Lawson was one of a kind. He didn't know why a woman like her didn't have a boyfriend or a husband. Brandt hadn't lived in Silver Lake when he met Callie, but Garrett remembered his sister saying she had dated little after moving to town. That begged the question…

What was wrong with the single men in town when there were such amazing women to date?

In Taryn's case, their loss was Garrett's gain.

Friends, yes.

But he would make the most of it while he was in Silver Falls.

AT LUIGI'S, GARRETT enjoyed the supreme combo pizza almost as much as Taryn's company. His stomach was full, and his mouth hurt from all the smiling. He'd laughed more tonight than he had in weeks. They never ran out of topics to discuss, though neither of them mentioned the booth or the bakery. It was as if the calendar had rewound to December. Only people wore fewer clothes, and nothing was decorated with red and green.

"Do you come here a lot?" he asked.

"Not as much as when I was younger. Now, I order takeout and watch TV at home." She patted the cardboard box filled with the leftovers. "I love having an extra meal for later."

The place was as she'd described—a casual, friendly restaurant where reservations weren't required. Booths with red vinyl seats lined the far wall, and they'd snagged one. Long tables with benches filled the rest of the place. No one appeared to mind sharing.

The only thing he'd change?

The noise level.

A soccer team of little girls, who called themselves the Silver Falls Angels, raced up and down the aisle, screeching and squealing about winning a game. Each had on the same blue and white uniform and matching socks. No halos, but several wore ponytails or headbands.

The volume hadn't reached eardrum-shattering levels yet, but the night was young, and a baseball team had arrived five minutes ago. Guys belched and swore as if they'd entered a bar full of salty patrons, not a pizza parlor over-flowing with kids.

Taryn laughed. "But who needs TV when entertainment and air-conditioning come with dinner here?"

He grinned. "Aren't I entertaining enough?"

"Yes." She winked. "I've tried but never been able to make a crust this good, so I like to figure out the secret. I asked Luigi to share the recipe, but he told me his mama would haunt him from her grave if he gave it to me."

"You'll have to make me a pizza so I can compare crusts."

"After the fair."

Yes! Another date. Except he'd better not say that aloud.

"Sounds good." Garrett wasn't only talking about the pizza. He enjoyed spending time with Taryn and wouldn't mind watching her cook. But tonight, more painting and decorating were on the agenda. They should probably go, so they weren't up too late again. "Are you ready to head home?"

"Let me finish my soda first." As she took a sip, a toddler ran past, chased by an older child. "I wonder if Callie and

Brandt will bring their children here."

Garrett held up his hands to stop Taryn. "Nope. No kids talk. It's hard enough thinking about my baby sister getting married. I'm not ready to imagine her being pregnant."

"Don't you want to be an uncle?"

He thought about it. "I'm Rex's uncle. At least that's how Callie told me to sign the tag on his Christmas gift."

Taryn laughed. "That sounds like your sister."

He nodded. "When I'm an uncle, I'll be the best one there ever was. Of course, I'll have to compete for the title with my brothers Flynn and Keaton."

"Callie mentioned you guys are competitive."

"We are, but not in a make-each-other-fail kind of way. We want the bragging rights."

"Those are important."

Taryn's hand lay on the tabletop. All Garrett had to do was move his hand forward a few inches, and they'd almost touch.

If this were a date—which it wasn't—he would cover her hand with his to see if her skin was as soft as he imagined.

Her hands were clean of paint, but had she put on lotion after washing them? If so, was it scented?

"So quick bright things come to confusion," a male voice said.

Taryn glanced up and stiffened.

That put Garrett on guard.

The man standing next to their table appeared to be in his early thirties. He wore a button-up shirt, tie, and dress pants. He held a pizza box. "Stop kidding around. You know that one."

Taryn's lips pursed. "I don't know what you're talking about, Nick."

Nick, as in Nick Baxter, who was Brandt's nemesis? Garrett took a closer look. Baxter's expensive watch seemed out of place for Luigi's and the town. But then again, Brandt said the guy was a tool. He was overdressed for a small-town pizza parlor, too.

Nick smirked. "I quoted a line of Shakespeare."

She took a sip of soda, visibly unimpressed. "You enjoyed doing that in high school."

"I did." The guy's chest puffed. If he noticed Garrett at the table, Nick didn't acknowledge him. "Though surprised you remember, given how you're Team Brandt these days."

"I didn't take sides," she said with more patience than Garrett would have managed around the guy. "I'm friends with both of you."

"Not true." Nick's gaze darkened. "You're baking Brandt's wedding cake after he wouldn't help me in December with that company in Raleigh."

"You've got to be kidding." She half laughed. "I work at a bakery. That's what we do. Bake cakes."

Nick wagged his eyebrows. "And now, there's more than one bakery in the area."

"Summit Ridge didn't open until March. Brandt and Callie hired me in January."

"Which is why you should have told them no when they asked," Nick said in a matter-of-fact tone. "You were a close friend, but you crossed the line. Now you pay."

Her lips parted. "So opening the other bakery is some sort of payback?"

Nick shrugged, but he didn't appear indifferent or confused. "If you wanted to remain neutral, you should have pulled a Switzerland. Now you'll pay."

The guy sounded more snake than human. No, that wasn't fair to snakes.

Even if Garrett hadn't known the backstory of how Nick used the power of attorney Brandt had given him to sell their company's technology and shut down the place, Garrett wouldn't want anything to do with him. The guy gave off a negative, slimy vibe.

Nick's lip curled. "Rumor has it business is down at Lawson's Bakery."

Taryn didn't cower or look away. She squared her shoulders. "The new patio is a big hit."

"A little too late." Nick sounded bored. "Are you ready for the summer fair?"

"Almost." She motioned across the table. "This is Garrett Andrews, one of Callie's brothers. He's helping me with the final touches."

"Well, good luck." Somehow Nick made those words sound condescending. "May the best bakery win."

Taryn stiffened. "What do you mean?"

Nick snickered. "Oh, haven't you heard?"

"Heard what?" Taryn asked, appearing more uncomfortable by the second.

Garrett couldn't take it any longer. He covered her hand

with his.

Gratitude shone in her eyes.

"Mr. Jones doesn't have time to build a booth this year with his wife's knee replacement. We'd applied to be on the waitlist. Once they saw our design, the board gave us the hardware store's place."

Taryn's face paled. Her lower lip trembled. "I hadn't heard."

Garrett squeezed her hand, wanting to reassure her and let her know she wasn't alone.

"It'll be the battle of the bakeries this weekend." The glee in Nick's voice matched his expression. "We're excited and raring to go. Spoiler alert! Our booth will be hard to beat."

She swallowed. "Good luck."

The woman had more class in her pinky finger than Nick Baxter had in his entire body because Garrett would have said something else to the guy. Words not meant to be spoken in a family restaurant. But this wasn't his fight...yet.

Nick barely glanced his way. "Nice to meet you, Barrett."

"Garrett."

"Whatever," Nick mumbled. "Take pains. Be perfect."

With that, he walked out, leaving a stench in his wake. Okay, it was pepperoni, but without the pizza, it wouldn't have smelled.

Taryn rubbed her face. "Did that really happen?"

"Unfortunately, yes." Garrett kept his hand on top of hers. "Do you think he's lying?"

"I have no idea, but what was he saying about pains and

perfect made no sense."

"It sounds like another quote." Reluctantly, Garrett raised his hand from hers. He typed the words into the search bar. The results sent his heart dropping.

She leaned forward. "What does it say?"

"It's a quote."

"Shakespeare?"

Garrett nodded. "From *A Midsummer Night's Dream*."

"It has to be a coincidence." Despite her words, she didn't sound convinced.

He readied his thumbs. "What was the first thing he said?"

"Bright confusion. Something like that."

Garrett typed. "'So quick bright things come to confusion' is also from *A Midsummer Night's Dream*."

Lines creased her forehead. She pushed away from the table. "I need to know what's going on. Margot will know."

He grabbed the pizza box. "Let's go."

# Chapter Ten

A T MARGOT'S, TARYN sat next to Garrett. She couldn't believe what Nick had said was true. The Summit Ridge Bakery *was* taking part in the summer fair. Talk about a worst-case scenario—a real-life nightmare. She had to do something, but what?

Her nerve endings stood on end, and her hands shook. "How did this happen?"

Margot sat in a chair opposite them. "We had several backup applications. When Mr. Jones pulled out earlier today, the board called an emergency meeting tonight. Nick must have gone from there to Luigi's."

Taryn stared at the carpet, unable to think straight. "Additions have been made in the past, but never a direct competitor to a First Avenue business."

"I'm so sorry, dear," Margot said, her voice full of compassion. "If it's any consolation, I voted no."

Taryn's gaze jerked up. "The others all voted yes."

It wasn't a question because that was the only way the board would have given Mr. Jones's slot to the other bakery. So much for having friends in the association. Still, it surprised her. Some had been in business as long as her father. But they were probably the ones also driving to Summit Ridge for their baked goods.

"The booth's design swayed others," Margot explained. "I must admit to being impressed."

Taryn's stomach churned, making her wish she'd skipped dinner.

"Let me guess," Garrett chimed in. "*A Midsummer Night's Dream.*"

Margot's mouth gaped. "How did you know?"

Garrett looked at Taryn. "Do you want to tell her?"

"I'll show you." Taryn pulled out her phone and showed Margot what they'd been working on. "This is Lawson's Bakery booth."

Margot's eyes widened. "It's almost the same design, except the Summit Ridge Bakery's booth has four sides. Yours only has three."

Taryn's insides twisted. She hadn't been paranoid thinking they wanted to put Lawson's Bakery out of business, but Nick had confirmed that earlier. But to stoop this low...

Her throat tightened. "My original design had four. I changed it because I didn't have enough time to build it that way."

"Did anyone see your booth before you put it into the storage shed last year?" Garrett asked.

Her mom and dad had been traveling in their RV in August and September. No one had been at her house. "No one."

Margot rubbed her chin. "How would they have gotten hold of your design?"

Taryn remembered. "The office bulletin board. I put the design up a few weeks ago so I could make a plan for baking the edible decorations."

"That must be how they found them," Margot said.

Taryn shook her head. "No one goes into the office except employees."

Silence filled the room. Both Garrett and Margot stared at her with knowing expressions.

"No." Taryn jumped to her feet. None of the guys who worked for her would do that. It was unthinkable. Impossible. "The employees who now work at Summit Ridge weren't around when I hung the designs. No one would do that. They wouldn't."

"It's difficult to think of someone close to us betraying our trust." Margot's voice was full of compassion. "But didn't you mention the other bakery has been copying your recipes? And when you introduce something new, they do, too."

"Yes, but..." Taryn plopped onto the couch. "Who would do this?"

"Who works at Lawson's now?" Margot asked.

"Jayden, Carl, Finley, and Brecken." It couldn't be one of them. She wanted to cover her ears, to stop them from ringing. "They aren't new employees. Carl worked under my dad before he retired."

Taryn's eyes stung, and she buried her face in her hands. This wasn't happening.

An arm went around her, and Garrett pulled her against him. She leaned into him, needing his support.

He rubbed her back. "We'll sort this out. I promise."

"But the fair." Oh, no. She squeezed her eyes tight before opening them. "I can't have the same theme as the other bakery. I'll be accused of copying them because people know my original booth was destroyed."

"Let's not panic, but it's Wednesday night," Margot reminded her. "You've already started over once."

Taryn wrapped her arms around her stomach, but that didn't stop the nausea. "I can't drop out."

"You need to come up with a different theme," Garrett said, his tone soft. "But one that will still work with the base part and the trees. The sign would be repainted, so it looked new."

Taryn rubbed her eyes. "A new sign is better than replacing everything else."

He squeezed her. "That's my girl."

Warmth furled inside her, making it not seem so bad. Nope, this wasn't the time to delude herself about what this was and wasn't. "All we need is to come up with a new theme and finish by Friday. Not exactly easy-peasy, but with a simple idea, it might work."

"Not you. We." Margot grinned. "Three brains are better than one."

"Let's brainstorm." Garrett kept his arm around Taryn, and she wasn't eager to scoot away. "We'll think of a theme tonight. Go shopping for what we need tomorrow morning and put the pieces together after that. You're not alone, but even if you were, you could do this."

Margot nodded. "Of course, you can."

"I appreciate the vote of confidence." Taryn didn't feel that way herself, but her family's legacy was at stake. Failing wasn't an option. "Let's do this."

GARRETT TOSSED AND turned all night. His brain wouldn't shut off. Not when he wanted to discover who helped Nick Baxter and the Summit Ridge Bakery drive Lawson's out of business. But an investigation would have to wait until booth version 3.0 was complete.

Despite his lack of sleep, Garrett needed to get busy. He arrived at the hardware five minutes before it opened. He wasn't surprised Taryn was here. The circles under her eyes matched his, but she might not appreciate being called twinsies over it.

"Hey," he said. "Ready to get this done?"

Her nod lacked enthusiasm, but she must be reeling since last night. She showed him a note on her phone. "I made a list of items, but I still can't think of what to call the booth."

"What was Margot's suggestion?"

"She had two." Taryn tapped on her screen and read. "A picnic for two or a summer picnic. They're not bad."

"But it's not as catchy as *A Midsummer Night's Dream*. I'll make another sign, but you can wait to paint it until you have a theme name you're happy with."

"Good plan. It's not as if we don't have other things to do."

When the doors opened, Taryn handed a list to Mr.

Jones. "If you could cut wood to these sizes while we shop, I'd appreciate it."

Garrett grabbed a cart. He had no idea what she'd spent to make the first two booths, but this theme didn't need as many items. Still, items filled the basket.

"Too bad the heavy building is done, or I'd need one of these." A leather tool belt caught his eye. He reached for it and put it on. "What do you think?"

She studied him. "Not exactly what I'd imagine a lawyer wearing, but it works."

"It does." He struck a pose.

Taryn laughed. "Next time."

He debated buying it now because there wouldn't be a next time. Unfortunately.

That bummed him out. Not about the tool belt, but spending more time with Taryn. After tomorrow afternoon, he'd have no reason to see her. Besides, he would fly home a week from Sunday.

After she paid, he loaded the supplies into the trunk before getting into her car.

The lines around her mouth had relaxed a little. That pleased Garrett.

She checked her phone. "That's the first thing on our to-do list."

"What's our next stop?"

"The general store." She started the car. "We may be able to get all the items, but if not, the market will have the rest."

Her voice sounded stronger than it had last night, but Garrett sensed a hesitation in her.

"You're doing great." He touched her shoulder. "It's going to be okay."

"I tell myself that, but I also keep thinking about how my dad will react when he sees how much money we've lost." Taryn pulled away from the curb and drove along Main Street. She kept her gaze focused on the road. "If I don't win the booth competition, which doesn't seem likely now, he'll be so disappointed in me. Again."

"That's a tough place to be."

She glanced his way for a moment. "Sounds like you've been there yourself?"

Tension formed between Garrett's shoulder blades. Few people knew what happened all those years ago, but hearing what he went through might help Taryn. He wanted to make her feel better and didn't know what else he could do.

"I have." He took a breath, not wanting to relive his biggest failure but knowing he should for her sake. "The summer after my first year of law school, I interned for my dad's law firm. I always assumed I'd work there and rake in six figures straight after I graduated with my JD. I was the definition of cocky."

"And you're not now?" she teased.

He laughed. "I'll take the Fifth."

"Sorry, I couldn't stop myself. Continue."

Garrett appreciated the reprieve. He took another breath. *Come on. It wasn't that bad.*

Except it changed the path of his life.

He swallowed. "My dad wanted one of us to follow in his footsteps. Flynn was in medical school, making our mom proud, and I was happy to apply to law school, knowing my career would be set working for the firm where he was a partner."

She tilted her head but didn't look his way. "Didn't you work for the DA's office?"

"I did after I graduated and passed the bar. This was before."

"Okay, but that's a completely different career path and income level."

Garrett blew out a breath. "You're not wrong."

"What changed?"

A perfectly valid question and the point of his story. "I made a mistake during that summer internship. Something that could have cost my dad's firm a lot, including their reputation."

Taryn gripped the steering wheel. "You were just an intern."

"But I should have known better." The words flew out. It was his standard reply. "I was a founder's son. I believed I knew what I was doing. It was a perfect example of hubris, and I'm sure I'm still used as an example for interns today. Not by name."

"What happened?"

"I was in preparing documents for the court. But I'd messed up, and some things slipped through. Thankfully, a senior attorney caught the mistake, even though I'd told him it wasn't necessary. If he hadn't thought to check..." Garrett scrubbed his face. "He submitted corrected paperwork. But the mistake was all on me. The next summer, I didn't return."

"Was it your choice?"

This was the part that sucked. "No, it was my dad's."

"Oh, Garrett." She touched his hand. "I'm sorry."

"Thanks." His throat hurt, but that was nothing new when he thought about this, which wasn't as often these days. "As a founding partner, my dad didn't want any sign of nepotism. He suggested I find a different internship the next summer. To gain a broader experience were his exact words. What he meant was stop riding his coattails and prove myself, so I did."

"Did you apply to his firm after you graduated?"

"No."

"Why not?"

"I still felt as if I needed to redeem myself, so I didn't send in my résumé. It was the right decision because my dad never told me to apply or asked my plans."

"That had to hurt after what you thought would happen."

He shrugged. That was a long time ago, but the sting remained. "I took a job at the district attorney's office. It was hard work, but I learned so much. After a few years, I struck out on my own. I did well enough my reputation grew. A top firm came calling, and I said yes. That's when higher-profile cases started coming my way."

"And here you are today, a partner in another firm. Which I'm guessing is what you wanted at your dad's firm."

Garrett sat taller. "Pretty much."

"So modest."

"No, attorneys are some of the most arrogant people you'll meet, including me."

She laughed. "Arrogant or not, you proved yourself."

He half laughed. "I did. The mistake I made as an intern made me a better attorney, a more paranoid one, and wealthier than I'd be if I'd taken that original path. Between you and me, I make more than my dad does."

"Okay, so not modest," she joked. "But it all worked out."

Garrett hadn't thought about it like that. "It did. And my dad is proud of me."

"He'd be crazy not to be." She parked a block off Main Street. "Your stories reaffirm something I've been telling myself."

"What's that?"

"Things happen for a reason."

"They do. I couldn't see that when I was an intern, but everything worked out the way it was supposed to."

"I hope my dad is as proud of me someday as yours is."

"He will be. So hang in there," Garrett encouraged, but her dimples didn't appear. "You're doing the best you can right now. Your dad will see it, and he'll be proud of you for how you're handling a tough situation."

# Chapter Eleven

IN HER BACKYARD, Taryn stared at the booth. It was finally coming together. Her dream of finishing on time had replaced her goal of winning. Not what she hoped for, but that didn't change the reality of the situation. Her original design might win, but the bakery—at least, Lawson's Bakery—wouldn't reap any benefits.

Sweat dripped down her spine, but they'd already taken a lunch break. She should do more before heading inside for a few minutes to enjoy the air-conditioning. But she would love an iced drink that wasn't water.

*Soon.*

Taryn glanced at Garrett, who removed the fairy lights that were no longer needed. Those would go into white tulle to resemble clouds instead.

Sweat dampened his hair. His skin gleamed. Muscles flexed as he moved pieces to give himself more room to work.

A sigh welled inside her.

*Look away.*

She did because admiring eye candy was one thing but focusing on him and sneaking one peek after another wasn't healthy. Not when she needed to focus on the task at hand.

*Repaint the sign.*

That would help the booth more than crushing on Garrett.

Wait. Taryn didn't have a crush. She found him attractive. Any breathing woman would.

"Knock. Knock." Raine Hanover walked from the side yard toward her. She carried a drink tray with two cups with straws sticking out. "I thought you might enjoy an iced coffee."

Taryn set her paintbrush on the edge of the can before standing. "Did you read my mind?"

Raine grinned. "No, but it's a scorcher, and these have been the drink of choice today."

"Thank you." Garrett stood and took the drink. "I met you in December."

Raine asked, handing a drink to Taryn, "Garrett, right?"

He nodded before taking a sip. "Hits the spot perfectly."

Taryn drank from hers. The cold plastic cup cooled her hand. "I owe you."

"I'll accept payment with baked goods," Raine joked.

"Done." Taryn sipped. "You're off early today."

Raine's lips drew into a thin line. "Emmett is stopping by."

Uh-oh. Based on Raine's expression, she didn't look thrilled about talking to her on-again, off-again boyfriend. But something made little sense. "He's in town on a Thursday?"

She rolled her eyes. "Emmett rented a room in a house, but he's moving into an apartment and wants his stuff I stored in my garage. I'll be running between the fair and the coffee shop all weekend, so I told him this weekend wasn't a good time. And then he showed up today unannounced."

Garrett drank more. "I'm going to keep working. Thanks for the coffee."

Taryn waited until he was over by the booth. "Are you okay?"

"I was a mess at first, but it's been over three months so I'm better."

She flinched. "That long?"

Raine nodded. "You've been dealing with the other bakery."

"I'm sorry for not being a better friend."

"Don't be. Summit Ridge stole your employees and is ruining your business. If that happened to me, I'd barely be functioning."

Taryn sheepishly raised her hand.

"Exactly, so don't think you failed as a friend. You haven't," Raine said in a matter-of-fact tone. "Honestly, all you would have done is listen to me go from one extreme to the other. We've tried long-distance, broke up, tried the long-distance again."

"Being apart and dating must be rough." Which was why that hadn't been an option when Garrett had been here over the holidays.

"The worst," Raine agreed. "And we can't ignore the bottom line. He hates living in a small town and only stayed because we started dating, but now he wants me to move to Seattle."

Taryn's jaw dropped. "Are you considering it?"

"No way." Raine's tone was firm. "My business and life are in Silver Falls. I looked at what's available, and I can't afford a coffee shop there. Now that I own a place, I don't want to be a barista or manager for someone else again."

"I'm sorry."

"Me, too, but I'm tired of this yo-yoing. I'd rather move on than keep pretending this will somehow miraculously work itself out. We want different things. That's no one's fault."

"I'm not sure I'd be handling this as well as you are."

"Oh, I wasn't at first, but I've had months to come to terms with it. I visited him in Seattle several times, and I don't want to move to a bigger city. There's a reason I bought a coffee shop in a small town. Silver Falls is home now."

Raine's cell phone buzzed. "That's probably Emmett, wondering where I am."

"Thanks again for the coffees."

"You're welcome." Raine surveyed the yard. "I can't wait to see your booth tomorrow. Someday, I'll get more creative with an entry."

"If you ever need ideas, ask."

"Trust me. I will." Raine laughed. "See you around, Garrett. Give my best to your sister."

"Will do." Garrett raised his cup. "I'll be by for another of these."

"Now, go work so you can sleep tonight." A quick hug and Raine left through the side gate.

"Raine seems nice." Garrett placed his glass against his neck.

"She is." Taryn glanced toward the side yard.

"You're worried about her."

"Yes, but I also feel guilty for not being a better friend. I've been so wrapped up in what's going on with the bakery—"

"I overheard what Raine said about that. Don't take this on, too."

"You're right." And he was. "Thanks."

"Any ideas for the name yet?"

Taryn shook her head. "Still hoping inspiration hits."

"Paint the sign and see what happens."

She raised a brow. "The egotistical attorney is getting bossy."

He winked. "Whatever it takes to finish."

On time was unspoken but implied.

Taryn picked up her paintbrush. "Whatever it takes."

AS THE SUN sank toward the horizon, Taryn sat, stifling another yawn. The tarp didn't provide any cushion for her knees, but it was better than nothing. Her body yearned for sleep—even a nap would do—but so many items remained on her to-do list. This last night before the fair began was crunch time.

"Looks good," he said.

"Thanks." She added the final coat of paint to the sign's frame. A cute yet catchy booth name eluded her. It appeared

"Summer Picnic" would win by default.

Not surprising when she was running on fumes. Raine's iced coffee had kept Taryn going, but she needed more caffeine.

"It's coming together," he said.

Not trusting her voice—which was becoming a habit—she nodded.

They had worked all day. Her tiredness coupled with the growing stress was catching up to her.

She lowered her paintbrush. Would all this work be for nothing?

*Push through it.*

The three words became her mantra. If she didn't do that, she would regret it.

Sleep would come. Not until Sunday night when the fair was over, but that was okay.

So much was at stake. She needed to keep the bakery going. It was her grandparents' legacy. Her parents', too.

Would it be hers?

Probably best not to think about that when she could erupt into tears at any moment.

Taryn could do this.

No, she *would* do this, and she wasn't alone.

She glanced at Garrett, who'd worked by her side all day. Okay, sometimes he'd been across the yard, but having him there kept her going as had her friends. Raine with the drinks and Callie, who'd delivered a dinner from the Falls Café before going to Margot's house to make wedding favors with her mom. And Jayden had left cookies on her doorstep on his break. Thank goodness for her friends, or Taryn might lose it.

She'd been on the verge since last night.

*Push through it.*

That was all she could do.

Garrett stuck fake daisies and greenery through the artificial grass that now covered the front panel. "You okay?"

It was strange how he sensed when she was struggling. "I can't think of any other booth names."

"We'll come up with something." His confidence gave her another boost. "We're almost finished with the rebuild, and once we are, that'll take some pressure off."

"You're right. I'll stop brainstorming." She surveyed the piece he worked on. Who knew a high-powered trial lawyer had mad building and craft skills? But... "Don't forget, part of the red and white checked tablecloth will cover the middle part of the front panel."

"I remember. That's why I'm doing the sides first. Once the cloth is on, I'll see what holes show." He grinned at her, and her pulse picked up. "I'm glad you bought two tablecloths. I thought it was overkill, but now I understand the method to your madness."

"This is the definition of madness." She half laughed. It was better than crying. But Taryn didn't have to force a fleeting smile. "You can't be too careful when you're down to the eleventh hour. I enjoy picnics, so I'll use the extra one for myself if we don't need both."

He glanced at the time. "We have sixteen hours until we have to be at the park."

Whenever he said "we," she muttered a little prayer of gratitude for him. "We should make it."

"Not should. We will make it."

"We will," she repeated, touching up a spot on the frame. "And then we celebrate."

"You know what would taste good right now?"

Taryn took a shot in the dark. "Something sweet from Lawson's Bakery."

"That's a given, but I was thinking more of a slice of juicy, chilled watermelon."

"Oh, yes." She thought about the one they'd bought earlier that morning. "There's a seedless one sitting on my kitchen counter, but it's not chilled."

"I can't believe I'm saying this, but it's for your display, not to eat."

"Spoilsport." Taryn pictured what was in her fridge. "I have a blueberry cheesecake or a marionberry pie."

"Oh, I'd love a slice of pie."

From watermelon to pie, though, she also had cake and pizza. Each one was a slice of goodness.

Her breath hitched. "A slice."

"What?"

Tingles erupted in her stomach.

"A slice of goodness, a slice of sweetness, a slice of summer." She nearly jumped to her feet. "A Slice of Summer. That's the name of our booth."

"A Slice of Summer." Garrett nodded. "I like it."

"Me, too." She pictured the words on the sign. "I can use a script font and add summery icons like a pie."

"Watermelons."

"Strawberries."

"Lemonade."

She had to think for a moment. "Ice cream."

"All fit the picnic theme, though ice cream melts."

"Not if you bought it in the park from the ice cream cart and ate it right away sitting on the grass."

"Works for me." His face brightened. "The name makes you happy."

Taryn nodded. "Version 3.0 isn't what I imagined the booth being thanks to the Summit Ridge Bakery, but it'll work."

"Of course, it will. You're an artist, Taryn. With cakes and other desserts, but also with your eye for design. You're talented enough to take any theme, including a summer picnic, and turn it into something memorable."

Heat balled at the center of her chest and spread outward. "Thank you, but I couldn't have done this without you. Even the name came from you."

He cleared his throat. "Speaking of which, aren't I supposed to get a slice of pie?"

"You are." She stood, brushing her hands together. "Do you want to eat it inside or outside?"

"In the house where it's cooler."

A few minutes later, they sat at the kitchen table with tall glasses of iced tea and slices of marionberry pie. "I can't believe I'm out of ice cream."

"No ice cream necessary." He scooped up another bite. "Marionberries are my new favorite berry, and the crust is perfect."

Flutters filled her stomach. She enjoyed it when Garrett complimented her cooking, but... "You have a spot of filling above your lip."

He wiped with a napkin on the left side. "Here."

She pointed to her face. "On the right. Your left."

Garrett wiped the other side, but it was still there.

Taryn hadn't used her napkin yet, so she came closer and patted above the corner of his mouth. "There."

His gaze met hers, and she froze. They were so close if she leaned forward, her lips would be against his.

Her heart slammed against her rib cage.

No, she couldn't... Could she?

A hundred thoughts ran through her mind. Tonight wasn't a date. Garrett was here as a friend to help her and leaving after Callie's wedding.

*Step away.* That was the smart thing to do. Except...

A connection flowed between them once again, stronger than before, pulling her closer, like two magnets.

She couldn't resist.

No, that wasn't one hundred percent correct.

Taryn didn't want to resist. She never took the last cookie or piece of dessert. Not even as a kid. But tonight... tonight she wanted to be greedy.

Take instead of giving.

That should frighten her more than it did.

Her lips parted, an invitation or a plea, but she didn't want to wait. Oh, logically, she should, but she was tired of always doing what she should do. If he would kiss her...

Except he hadn't moved.

Desire flared in his eyes, matching the way she felt inside.

Taryn closed the short distance between them, pressing her mouth against him. They'd kissed before, albeit months ago, but something about this was more like a first kiss.

It might be the season, summer instead of winter, but he tasted sweeter than she remembered.

Like the pie.

Forget marionberry. He was now her new favorite. She'd never thought of warmth as a flavor, but there it was, with a hint of salt. Most likely from being outside in the heat.

His arms remained at his sides and hers, too. She gripped the napkin in her right hand.

If Taryn touched him, she might not want to let go.

That would be a mistake.

She lost track of time, but slowly his lips lifted from hers.

A chill ran through her. Goose bumps pricked her skin. Not from the air-conditioning, but from him ending the kiss.

Taryn bit her lip.

Garrett's pupils were wide. His breathing unsteady. "Kissing you was better than I remember."

A hundred times better. But she didn't know if she could speak coherently at the moment, given how much his kiss affected her.

She nodded, trying to pull herself together, hoping her heart rate slowed.

"Why haven't we been doing this the entire time?" he asked.

"Friends," she croaked.

"We are friends." He ran the edge of his fingertip along her jawline. His touch was light, and his speed nearly slow-motion. "But we could be more."

A thrill shot through her. She wanted that, but...

Memories of December flashed. A rush of heartwarming images and overwhelming emotions from January followed. Like then, he would leave to return home to a job that required his full attention. And she would be here, working just as hard at the bakery. Well, hopefully.

Once again, this wasn't the right time for...

More.

Taryn jumped to her feet. "I'll put the plates in the dishwasher, so we can finish the booth."

"Hey." He held her hand. "What just happened?"

"Stuff is in my head."

"New stuff?"

"Old stuff."

Realization dawned on his face. "From my last visit."

She nodded.

"Want to tell me about it?" His tone wasn't pushy.

"Not really, but I should." She took another breath. That didn't calm her. She wiped her clammy palms against her shorts, destroying the napkin still in her hand, but she felt a little better, so totally worth it. "This is embarrassing."

"Life is full of embarrassing moments. They're only as bad as we make them."

That was true. She would try again. "Remember when I told you my reason for reacting the way I did when you came to the bakery the first time and then later that night?"

"I remember." His Adam's apple bobbed. "You didn't appreciate being dismissed so easily."

She nodded, surprised he remembered. "I thought of that happening again."

Garrett sat ramrod straight, his shoulders squaring as if ready to spring into battle.

*Oh, no.* He was taking this the wrong way.

Taryn took a seat. "Not by you. It has nothing to do with you. It's me. And my parents. Well, my dad. He makes me feel so inadequate. I hate feeling I'm less."

"I'm sorry I made you feel that way, too. I won't repeat my mistake. I'm not like your father. I see how smart you are and how hard you work to make the bakery a success. You are more than enough."

His words filled her up the way his kisses had. "Thank you."

"I don't want to go back, but I would like to move forward. As friends, we can call ourselves that this week, and as two people attracted to each other." Garrett's tone was full of compassion. He squeezed her hands. "And are equals."

She wet her swollen lips. "Logically, I know I'm not less, but a part of me can't let go of those thoughts. I mean, he's my dad."

"You want to make him proud."

"So much." Her shoulders sagged. "But I'm afraid I can't. And if that's the case, I should let it go and do my own thing, whatever that might be. Ever since I was little, I dreamed about making the bakery my own. Not to erase the past, but to build upon it for the next generation of customers. I have so many ideas. A vision board. Plans."

"I'd love to see them sometime."

Heat pooled on her face. The designs were in the office, but no one had ever asked her about them, including her father. "That has nothing to do with kissing you."

"You wanted to kiss."

No sense in denying the obvious. She nodded. "But I got scared. You and the bakery have become entwined in my mind. The patio was doing well, and the booth thing happened. Now, we've rebuilt a new theme, and we kissed."

"You're waiting for the next shoe to drop."

"And prove my dad has been right all along that I'm not capable."

Garrett held her hands in his. "Your dad must be a decent guy, or he wouldn't have such a wonderful daughter like you. But he's wrong. You won't prove anything other than you're capable and exactly what Lawson's Bakery needs to thrive. If kissing makes you feel—"

She kissed him hard against the lips. "Kissing you makes me feel good. But I freaked out a little. Or a lot."

"You've had a rough week." Garrett raised her chin with his fingers. "Please know, I'm not here to make you feel bad or hurt you. Our situations haven't changed since December, and you heard your friend mention trying to date long-distance."

Taryn nodded. "I don't want that."

"Me, either." His tone was soft and his gaze compassionate. "What I do want is to help you. I also want you to see the beautiful, creative, intelligent woman I see, okay?"

She nodded, wanting that, too.

"It's my turn." He lowered his mouth to hers, pressing gently, almost teasing. "Now, let's finish the booth because we have a long weekend ahead of us."

Her pulse skittered. "Us."

He flashed her a lopsided grin. "You don't think I'm going to let you have all the fun at the fair by yourself, do you?"

# Chapter Twelve

"YOU NEED TO sleep." Garrett didn't have to glance at the time to know it was late. Taryn kept yawning. She would fall asleep sitting up if they kept going. He also wanted to kiss her good night. That had been on his mind since they locked lips earlier. He'd glimpsed her dimples, but he wanted more. "We're pretty much finished."

"It's the 'pretty much' that worries me." As she studied each section, she stifled another yawn. "I want to make sure we haven't forgotten anything."

"The only missing pieces are the baked goods."

"Jayden texted me photos. The guys have those under control."

Garrett figured as much based on the notifications buzzing on her phone tonight. "That means there's no reason not to call it a night."

Still, she hesitated. Taryn rubbed her arms. The temperature had dropped.

"Something's on your mind." He wanted to know what.

"Nerves," she admitted, but she didn't lower her arms. "I pinned my hopes on the patio opening and winning the booth competition. Now…"

"You don't know what's going to happen."

"No, but a worst-case scenario litany is playing on an endless loop in my head."

"You need to sleep."

"I know." She sighed. "Otherwise, I'll be like the walking dead for the next three days."

"You don't want to scare the small children."

Taryn grimaced. "That's not the type of picnic or slices we want people to associate with Lawson's Bakery."

"Though I bet they'd never forget it."

She laughed. "For sure, especially after the nightmares."

"That's why we won't let that happen."

"Sleep."

"Sleep." He walked toward her with purposeful steps. "No one knows what tomorrow or any day after that will hold. That's part of the fun."

She eyed him warily. "Says the trial attorney who preps nonstop for a big trial."

"Nothing wrong with preparing, which is what we've been doing, but at some point, you have to tell yourself you've given it your all and call it."

Her expression softened. "You'll be an excellent uncle someday."

Something in his chest shifted. He froze.

"Thanks." Garrett didn't know what else to say, which wasn't like him.

"I guess it's time for good night."

"It is." Except he would rather turn on a movie, cuddle on the couch, and kiss. Taryn, however, needed sleep more than she needed kisses. Unfortunately. "But I'll be here in the morning."

"I'll be ready."

He moved closer. All he wanted was to kiss her until the worry disappeared from her eyes. "Get some sleep."

"I might check—"

"No." He kissed her forehead. "Good night."

"Are you this bossy with your clients?"

"Worse. I tell them what to wear, how to sit, and what to say."

"Guess I'm lucky."

"The luckiest." He brushed strands of hair off her face. "You need to go inside and forget about stuff for the rest of the night."

And somehow, Garrett would do the same. But shutting down his brain and thoughts about Taryn wouldn't be easy-peasy tonight. "Text me when you're ready for me to come over tomorrow."

IN THE MORNING, Garrett woke early and took the dogs for a walk. His phone remained silent—no text notifications or calls from Taryn. She must have slept late. Good, because she needed it. Now, he wanted to make sure she didn't overdo it during the fair.

Not his job.

Not really.

But while she looked out for the bakery, someone needed to watch out for her. He was happy to take on the task.

"It's what friends do."

Sadie stopped sniffing a bush and glanced at him.

"What?" Garrett didn't appreciate the dog's head tilt. "We're friends. Friends kiss."

Sadie remained unconvinced. Another scent must have caught her attention because she stuck her nose against the grass.

"Fine, be that way."

He grinned, thinking about kissing Taryn again. But beyond kisses, he enjoyed being with her. Only next week would be crazy busy. At least they would have this weekend. His brothers arrived tomorrow, and they would help Callie. But come Monday, his sister's needs were his priority. Garrett prided himself on his time management skills. They would need to be dialed in if he was to see Taryn and not only at the wedding.

The dogs led him up the walkway to Margot's house. Their tails wagged faster.

He laughed at their excitement. "You guys know it's treat time."

Inside the entryway, he unclipped their leashes and hung them on hooks next to the door. They darted to the kitchen.

"Give Mama a minute, and I'll get your treats." Margot called to the dogs from the dining room, where she laid out a quilt.

"New project?"

"It's our booth's giveaway for the summer fair. Our theme is Homespun and Heartfelt." She ran a fingertip over the colorful fabric as if it were a precious work of art. "The employees at the quilt shop contributed squares, and I pieced them together. It turned out well."

"It's beautiful."

"Thanks. And thank you for taking Angus and Sadie on a walk. I'll drop them off at your sister's before I head over to the park."

"Do you need help?"

"No. My manager and her husband have it all covered. This is the first year I haven't done it myself, and I must admit it's a relief only to have to deliver the quilt and candy."

"Callie mentioned her booth would have dog biscuits and magnets to giveaway, but she didn't make it sound like she spent much time on it."

"Her theme is Dog Days of Summer. It'll be cute. Some First Avenue business owners put a lot of effort into their booths and windows at Christmastime. Others don't. Pippa, who recently purchased the flower shop, hasn't competed in an event, so everyone's curious about what she'll do."

"A dark horse."

"Exactly, but it's the perfect way for a florist to showcase their skills, so I expect Pippa won't disappoint. The same as Taryn with her summer theme."

"Given the circumstances, the bakery's booth turned out great." He took pride in that and contributed to her theme name, which he would let her unveil, but it was all Taryn. He was only an extra pair of hands. His smile grew. "She is amazing."

"You're sweet to help her."

"It's the least I can do while I'm here."

Margot's gaze sharpened. "Why is that?"

Oops. He didn't want to go there. "Taryn's employees need to be at the bakery. Her parents are out of town. She has no one else."

Margot wagged her finger. "Don't tell me you haven't noticed she's attractive, smart, and single."

He held up his hands. "I won't deny it, but it's no different from me walking the dogs or running errands for you."

She harrumphed. "Well, it should be."

That made him laugh. "No matchmaking."

"I remember, but I don't like it."

His cell phone buzzed. He glanced at it.

**Taryn:** *Awake. Guess I needed the rest.*

Garrett reread the message.

"That must be from Taryn, your friend." Margot emphasized the last word. "Based on the goofy grin on your face, you define friend differently than I do."

He wasn't about to answer that. The phone went into his pocket. "I have some time before I help her. Need anything done?"

"Now that you mention it, I'd love for you to take the dogs to Callie's. That'll save me a trip."

"I'll do that." He would also pick up coffees for them from Tea Leaves and Coffee Beans. Not iced ones this time. But the caffeine would be a nice pick-me-up to start what would likely be a long day.

But a good one. Any day he got to spend with Taryn

would be.

He only hoped the fair worked out the way she planned.

ON FRIDAY AT noon, Garrett helped Jayden load everything into a borrowed pickup truck. Taryn had left for the park with all the smaller décor pieces, ice chests, cases of water bottles, and other smaller items. "That should be all the booth parts."

"Great." Jayden closed the gate. "Carl is bringing the baked goods over."

"You guys are a well-oiled machine."

"Yep, and this is nothing compared to putting together a Christmas window. We start after we close on Saturday and work all day Sunday. But we finish, while others keep at it for a few days or more."

Garrett climbed into the passenger seat.

Jayden slid behind the wheel. "Thanks for helping Taryn. I didn't mean to give you a hard time."

"Yes, you did."

"Okay, fine, but she's like a sister to me."

"I get it. I do the same with Callie."

"Please be careful."

"We're friends." The words shot out a little too quickly, but Garrett didn't know if Jayden noticed.

"Friends can still hurt each other without meaning to."

"We've talked." And kissed before talking. "I won't make the same mistake again."

Though the ending would be identical after he returned

home. There was no way around that.

"Glad to hear it. I worry about her."

"Me, too." Garrett didn't know how much Jayden knew about Taryn's relationship with her parents, so he didn't want to bring it up. "But she's strong and smart. She'll figure this out."

Jayden turned the key in the ignition. The engine roared to life. "She is. And once things click into place, the Summit Ridge Bakery had better watch out."

The guy seemed on the level and caring, but someone was passing on info to their competitor. The question was, who?

Ten minutes later, they unloaded the pieces in the spot marked for Lawson's Bakery.

He glanced around at all the pop-tents and folded tables being set up in two rows with an ample space in between. "It doesn't look like much yet."

Jayden snickered. "Just wait. The booths will go up quickly, and soon, the aisle between them will be crowded. It'll stay that way each day. People enjoy the entertainment and the rides, but this part always gets a lot of traffic, too."

Jayden pulled out the pop-up tent from the case. "She ran to the bakery to help Carl get the next load. She'll be here soon."

Together, they put the tent in place. That not only marked their spot, but the canopy also provided shade. Garrett set up the table in the front. There was another, but he would wait for Taryn for that one.

"Look at all this stuff." Margot came up to them. She

wore a quilted vest with long fringe on the bottom. That would be cooler out in the temperature that hovered in the eighties today. "Impressive."

Garrett nodded. "It's just like our favorite baker."

"You mean me," Jayden teased.

Margot laughed. She appeared to have grown two, possibly three inches, and her face beamed brighter than a streetlight on Main Street. Her eyes twinkled. "You like her."

Garrett glanced around. "Who?"

Margot winked. "Taryn."

"Shhhh."

"I heard nothing." Jayden adjusted the pop-up tent legs.

"You tried fooling me this morning, but I see through 'friends.'"

"I don't know what you're talking about."

She raised her chin. "Nice try, but I always knew the two of you would be good together."

They were. Garrett's smile felt as if it was spreading wide enough to fall off his face. He'd had his reasons for not calling her before. But this time would be different. And friends, even ones who kissed occasionally, was better than nothing.

"Don't look now, but your favorite baker has arrived."

"Jayden's here," Garrett deadpanned.

Margot rolled her eyes. "Go make yourself useful and hug her nerves away. Better yet, kiss her."

With that, she turned and walked to her booth as if she were the queen bee of the hive. And in Silver Falls, Margot Winslow kind of was.

"It's coming together." Taryn carried a box. Nerves poured from her like heat waves off the asphalt.

A man dressed in white followed her with another box. That must be Carl, who she'd mentioned as a long-time employee.

Garrett wanted to do what Margot had said—hug and kiss Taryn—but he settled for touching her shoulder for now. "Now that you're here, we can put up all the fun decorations. It's going to be great."

She nodded, though it appeared as if she were trying to convince herself.

He squeezed. "It doesn't matter what happens when they announce the winner. You pulled this together when most people would have given up. You did it."

Taryn lowered her gaze almost shyly. "Not me. We did this. I couldn't have done this without you."

His chest swelled at her words. He wanted to do more for her—whatever she needed.

Jayden whistled. "Come on, you two. It's time to show off your hard work."

Garrett bumped his shoulder against hers. "Let's finish this."

She glanced at the other booths coming to life, but her expression didn't tell him if she worried about the other competitors or not. The Summit Bakery appeared to be on the opposite end from hers. That had to be a good thing rather than right next door.

Her smile was fleeting with no dimples, but at least it was there.

In his forties with thinning hair and a calm demeanor, Carl set his box on the table. "That's my cue to get out of here. Let me know when you run low on samples. I'll keep Finley and Brecken baking them, so we're set for the weekend."

"Thanks." Jayden slapped Carl's shoulder. "Be there soon. It'll be rough rotating between the bakery and fair with only five of us—"

"Six," Garrett chimed in. "I'll help, too. But I'm better suited for the booth."

Jayden's posture relaxed. "Even better."

"Yes. That'll be an enormous help." Taryn's grin made Garrett feel as if he'd given her a million dollars, not a few hours of his time. "The bakery's usually closed on Sundays, but today and tomorrow will be rough, so thanks."

"Whatever you need."

And he meant it. This was more than making amends.

He swallowed around the lump in his throat. He fought the urge to reach out to Taryn and touch her. Instead, he pressed his arms against his sides.

She took a deep breath. "Let's do this."

An hour in, Jayden returned to the bakery.

Two hours in, other business owners came by for first and second looks.

Three hours later, the final decoration—a baguette on top of a picnic basket—was in place.

Taryn rubbed her palms together. "I can't believe we finished early."

"Teamwork and a great plan." Garrett stepped away to

see how everything fit.

"A Slice of Summer" theme was, in a word, summery. The red, white, and blue color scheme with a yellow splash from the daisies worked well with the trees on either side and the artificial grass on the table and front panel. A picnic basket and tiered serving plates filled with samples: watermelon-slice-shaped cookies, cake slices, pie slices, and slices of bread sat on the table next to a large glass drink dispenser full of ice water with slices of lemon floating in it.

"You put out all the sample slices."

"I wanted to for the judging. Saturday and Sunday, I'll rotate them."

"Bravo." Margot applauded. "The theme is quaint with a hint of nostalgia, a perfect combination for Lawson's Bakery."

Taryn's dimples appeared. Her face lit up. "Thank you. I appreciate your help."

"You did this." Margot didn't miss a beat. "Your parents will be proud of you."

She stood a little taller. "I couldn't have done it without Garrett."

Margot's twinkling gaze traveled between him and Taryn. "It's nice you have such a good friend."

But the mischievous expression on Margot's face suggested she wanted to say more. Garrett was happy she didn't.

"Very nice," Taryn agreed.

Margot leaned closer. "Your trees and front panel are a hundred times better than Summit Ridge's."

Garrett nodded. "I thought the same thing."

"They might win. And I'm okay with that. But so much for my Midwinter Night's Dream window for December," she joked.

Taryn would be okay. No matter how the judging turned out. "What about Twelfth Night?"

"I'll add it to the list," she said.

"No one knows what will appeal to people," Margot said in that wise tone of hers. "But Pippa's Summer Blooms theme is impressive for a newbie."

Taryn glanced in the direction of the florist's booth, but there had to be eight to ten other booths before that one. "I need to check it out."

He put his arm around her. "Go now. I'll stay here."

"When the ice cream booth opens, we'll celebrate. The parlor is giving out mini cones for their samples."

"Sounds like a plan." And he had another one for when they finished tonight.

A date.

Well, dinner.

They would both need it after working so hard. And he wanted this time with Taryn to last as long as it could.

# Chapter Thirteen

"I HOPE YOU enjoy the slice of apple pie." Taryn stood behind the booth's table and handed a napkin to a man. The summer fair usually drew people from surrounding towns, but his Summit Ridge University tank top made her wonder if he was here to support the other bakery.

Paranoid much?

The answer was yes.

Which was why the less she said about his town, the better.

As she held in a laugh, she pulled a coupon from her apron pocket and gave it to him. "Lawson's Bakery is around the corner from the park. We're open tonight if you want to redeem your coupon for more pie or any other sweet treats. The coupon is valid through next Saturday night."

Taryn had memorized the spiel after saying it a few times. She hoped the limited time frame brought in more customers. The only expense was the paper to print them on—Brecken's siblings had cut them in exchange for cookies—and less profit earned on items. But she would take the loss to get the baked goods in people's hands, er, mouths.

He placed the coupon in his pocket before picking up

the small plate and a fork. "Thanks."

As he walked away, she straightened the stack of napkins. Brecken worked behind her and made sure the supply of samples didn't run low. The only thing missing—Garrett.

After they'd eaten ice cream cones, he'd gone to Callie's booth to see if she needed anything, and he hadn't returned. The crowds blocked the stalls on the other side, but it was no big deal.

At least that was what she kept telling herself.

Garrett had done what he said he would do—help her complete the booth. Sure, he'd mentioned helping her this weekend, but who knew what that meant? A kiss changed nothing between them, even if she might want another one. Okay, a lot more.

Friends.

Friends who kiss.

But nothing else.

She brushed off a pang. That was the safest path.

Who was she kidding?

The only path.

Garrett would return home after Callie and Brandt's wedding, and Taryn had to save the bakery. A few kisses were all she could afford.

"Cute booth," Mrs. Sellwood, one of Taryn's former schoolteachers and the mother of Silver Falls's mayor, carried her little dog, Madden, who panted at the table of baked goods. "I've had my fill of sweets today, but I'll be here tomorrow for a slice from you. Clever theme."

"Thank you."

The woman had canceled Madden's days at Callie's Wags and Tails when the doggy daycare flooded, but she later apologized and returned. Now it appeared Mrs. Sellwood had done something similar to Lawson's Bakery. She used to come into the bakery a few times a week, but Taryn hadn't seen her in weeks. Possibly, months.

Her stomach knotted. This weekend would remind Taryn of the customers who no longer came into the bakery. "I haven't seen you lately. How have you been?"

"Watching my figure."

Or driving to Summit Ridge.

Taryn pressed her lips together. Customers were free to shop where they wanted, but she would try to remind them to visit Lawson's. That was what a business owner—or a future one—did.

"Good for you." She handed a coupon to Mrs. Sellwood. "If you need to satisfy your sweet tooth or want a fresh loaf of bread or rolls this week, here's a coupon for you."

"Thanks, dear. I love a bargain."

That explained why Mrs. Sellwood hadn't been in. "It's always good to get a deal."

"Yes, it is."

"Enjoy the fair." Taryn noticed people standing in line. "Callie has dog biscuits if Madden is hungry."

Mrs. Sellwood glanced over her shoulder. "We'll go there next."

A boy and a girl of around eight wearing matching yellow T-shirts, and a man came up to the table. The children stared at the cookies with wide eyes.

Taryn's grin widened. She recognized them from earlier. If she remembered right, they had moved to town recently, but she hadn't seen them in the bakery. She wanted to change that. "Back for more?"

He grinned at his kids, who appeared to hold their breaths. "They wanted another picnic cookie."

"That's fine. You're welcome to have more picnic cookies." Those last two words brought a tingle. As Taryn gave each child a napkin, an idea formed. What if she created special dessert menus for various events? Caterers did that, but customers might enjoy those, too. Words popped in her mind: picnic, kid favorites, romantic, chocolate lovers, no chocolate. She gave the dad a second coupon. "If you have two cookie eaters in the family, an extra one might come in handy."

He laughed. "It will. Thanks."

The father handed each child a cookie. "No more after this, or you'll get a tummy ache."

Both kids nodded before eagerly biting into their cookies.

Their smiling faces made the long hours preparing for the fair worthwhile. She'd been so focused on surviving, she forgot what she'd love about working at Lawson's—bringing smiles and creating memories with desserts. She needed to remember that. "Enjoy your time at Silver Falls Summer Fair."

The three walked away.

"I checked all the containers." Brecken refilled the empty platters before removing his gloves. He wore a Lawson's

Bakery apron over his clothes. "We're almost out of the watermelon cookies. Do you want me to call Jayden or get them myself?"

There'd been a steady flow of visitors to the booth but not overwhelming. "I can hold down the fort for a few minutes."

"I'll run." Brecken took off.

"Someone's in a hurry."

Her pulse kicked up. She turned to face Garrett. He'd changed into a different pair of shorts and a polo shirt. "Having fun?"

He nodded. "I helped Callie until Anna arrived. Ran to Margot's, showered, and changed. I also checked out the competition."

"Any favorites?"

"My sister's is cute. But I like yours."

"Ours," Taryn corrected. "This booth wouldn't have happened without you."

"Thanks." He glanced to his left. "Summit Ridge did an okay job with *A Midsummer Night's Dream*, but a few things are missing, so it feels incomplete from what you designed. The florist shop nailed hers. It's stunning."

"Pippa's impressed me."

A woman stood next to Garrett and took a slice of black forest cake. "These desserts are so creative."

"Thanks." Taryn handed her a coupon. "This is good through next Saturday if you want to see what else Lawson's Bakery offers."

"Thanks." She picked up a napkin. "It's hard to pick one

booth over another, so I'm doing a taste test to see who gets my vote."

Taryn's chest tightened. "Sounds like an excellent method. Enjoy the summer fair."

Garrett watched the woman walk away. "Nervous?"

"I was, but now I'm…" She searched for the word. "Resigned. From a purely aesthetic view, Pippa's booth should win. But even if it's Summit Ridge, that's okay. I—we did our best. Now, I'm doing what I can to draw attention to Lawson's and send customers that way. Only time will tell if it's enough."

"Great attitude."

She raised her chin. "Thanks."

"Any marionberry slices?"

Taryn laughed. "Your true motivation now comes out."

He winked. "Guilty, though I wanted to see how you were doing."

She handed him a plate, fork, and napkin. Pre-slicing the pieces made things easier and cleaner. The table behind her, where all the prep work took place, was another story. "So far, so good. Lots of traffic. Brecken is refilling samples for me."

"I wondered why you were alone."

"He'll return shortly."

"What are you doing after this?" he asked.

Her heart bumped. "Putting all the stuff away and washing the trays for tomorrow before getting a late dinner."

"Callie and Anna want pizza. We had it the other night, but do you want to join us?"

"I'll never say no to pizza."

"It's a date."

A thrill shot through her. She nodded. "I'm looking forward to it."

Probably too much, but she would deal with that later.

Four girls approached the table. They appeared to be around thirteen or fourteen with their world-is-ours-for-the-taking vibe. Each held a ballot and a short pencil.

The taller of the bunch rose on her tiptoes. "Oh, I like this one."

A redheaded girl with freckles nodded. "I love picnics. Someday I'll have a boyfriend, and we'll go on picnics every weekend."

A girl with glasses pointed at the tiered platter. "Look at the watermelon cookies. Those are so cute."

"Cake!" One in a flower print romper tugged on the taller one's arm. "We have to have a slice."

Another girl with short pink hair tapped her pencil against her chin. "Picnic. Flowers. I don't know which to vote for."

"My grammy says you can never go wrong with pie," the one with glasses said.

The romper girl nodded. "Pie or cake."

Garrett leaned toward her. "That's my cue to get out of the way. See you later."

The girls giggled and wanted to know about each dessert, so Taryn explained the different types and flavors. "You're free to take whichever you'd like. And here's a coupon you can use. I'll give you an extra one for your family."

The girls thanked her before walking away.

"I'm voting for this booth," the one in the romper said. "Nothing beats free—"

"Cake," the three others said at the same time, and all four burst out laughing.

Oh, to be that young again. Taryn's smile spread. She hoped the girls made the most of the next few years of high school together. Most of her girlfriends she'd grown up with had moved away from Silver Falls. It was a town to leave. That was why several First Avenue businesses belonged to new people in town. A few had returned after college like Nick, and others had left a second time as Brandt had done. She was grateful to have Callie, Anna, Raine, and now Pippa move to Silver Falls.

"Got everything." Brecken hurried toward the booth with a box. "Sorry it took so long, but the line is out the gate, so Jayden needed me."

"No problem." A line meant sales. "Things have been slowing down here. Restock everything and help out at the bakery. I'll call if I need you."

"Sure thing, Boss." Brecken pulled on gloves and opened the first container of cookies.

She greeted more visitors to the booth. As soon as Brecken refilled one type of dessert, they disappeared. But soon, they caught up.

"I sliced some extra cake and pie." He pulled off his gloves. "I'll be a phone call away."

"Thank you." The crowd had thinned. Many were at the food trucks and stands or the carnival rides. "Tell Jayden,

Carl, and Finley thanks."

"Will do, Boss." With that, Brecken headed toward First Avenue.

She straightened the table, even though the judging must end soon.

Anticipation shot to her toes. Taryn lowered her expectation of winning. But any kind of placement, including an honorable mention, would be better when she told her father what happened.

Not that she'd failed.

Taryn ran her fingertips along the fake grass covering the table. She'd succeeded by not giving up.

"Callie told me they'd be announcing the winner soon." Garrett stood in front of the booth. He peered behind her. "Are you still alone?"

"Brecken brought over more samples, but things are winding down here, so I sent him to the bakery to work there."

"I'll help you." He squeezed through the gap between the table and the tree covering the tent pole. "What do I need to do?"

She gave him some coupons. "Before people walk away, hand them a coupon."

"Easy-peasy."

"It is." She pulled disposable gloves from the box and handed him a pair. "Put these on in case you need to handle any of the plates or samples."

They worked side by side. More than once, Garrett sweet-talked people to visit Lawson's with a sales pitch that would have made her grandpa proud. "If being a lawyer doesn't work, you'd make a great salesperson."

"Only for something I love."

"It's all about the marionberry pie."

"What do you mean?" he feigned innocence.

"I saw you sneak a slice." Possibly two, but she wouldn't call him out on that extra one. He deserved it.

"My eating more pieces means less to pack up when you close the booth. I'm assuming the stuff either goes home with you or to the bakery."

"The bakery, and excellent save."

"Lawyers are known for their oratory skills."

"As in talking your way out of something."

"Exactly."

"Good evening," a woman announced over a sound system that broadcast through the park. "Thank you for attending Silver Falls Summer Fair."

The crowd cheered and clapped.

"We appreciate all who cast ballots for their favorite booth theme. This was a record-setting year for the number of ballots cast. And now, I'd like to announce the winners of our First Avenue Business Association Booth Competition," the voice said.

The people got quiet.

Taryn's muscles tensed.

Garrett put his arm around her.

"Honorable mention goes to Lawson's Bakery's: A Slice of Summer."

She released the breath she was holding. People and the

other business owners clapped.

"You okay?" Garrett whispered.

A nod was all she could manage. The bakery had placed. No, it wasn't a win, but she would take an honorable mention.

"Second place goes to Summit Ridge Bakery's *A Midsummer Night's Dream.*"

People clapped again. Someone whistled.

"At least they didn't win," Garrett whispered before brushing his lips over hers.

Taryn nodded.

"And the winner of this year's Summer Fair Booth Competition is Silver Falls Flowers's Summer Blooms."

People cheered.

Taryn clapped. "Pippa deserved it, but is it awful if I feel relieved?"

"Not at all." Garrett pulled her closer. "Given where we were on Wednesday night, I'd say honorable mention is a grand prize."

He was correct. She straightened. They'd pulled together a booth that not only finished early but also placed. "Me, too."

Five minutes later, the honorable mention ribbon hung from her sign.

*Except it's not first place.*

Her dad's voice echoed in Taryn's head. She'd upset him by helping Callie win the Christmas window contest when everyone in town believed she'd been a shoo-in to repeat as winner. No doubt he'd blame her for not winning. But neither he nor Grandpa had won, either.

She wouldn't let him get to her.

At least Summit Ridge hadn't won. No one had mentioned the similarities between the trees of the two booths. Though Raine had said the *Midsummer Night's* theme looked more like something she would make.

Ironic.

Was that the word?

All she knew was the joy of finishing the booth, spending time with Garrett, and kissing him again made not being able to speak up about her design being stolen worth it. And though a part of her wanted to say something, she wouldn't drag Lawson's into a bakery battle of he-said, she-said. No one would win without losing customers—something they couldn't afford during a business slump.

One bright side: Nick hadn't shown up to gloat. Taryn would take that as a part of her honorable mention prize.

"So what happens now?" he asked.

"When they announce the fair is closed for the night, that's our cue to clean up. Then we can eat."

"Hungry?"

She nodded, hoping her stomach didn't grumble. "I hope there's not too long a wait for the pizza."

"There won't be."

"You sound certain."

"I am because Brandt ordered ahead of time. Dinner will be delivered to Margot's house."

"Callie found a good guy."

"She did. I wasn't sure about him at first, but they fit

together. And he treats her well."

"Of course, he does. Brandt adores her. Your sister is crazy about him." Someday, Taryn would like to fall in love as Callie and Brandt had. "Relationship goals."

"If you wanted one."

Which he didn't. And neither did Taryn. At least that was what she kept telling herself.

But as Taryn stared at Garrett, she wasn't sure if that was one hundred percent true any longer.

# Chapter Fourteen

ON SATURDAY MORNING, Garrett carried Margot's quilt to her booth. Not a cloud was in the sky, and the temperature was warming already. A perfect summer day for a fair to celebrate the season, but it would be hot later. Tall trees in the park provided some shade, as would the tents covering the booths, but it was sunglasses, hat, and water bottle kind of weather.

"Can you and Brandt hang the quilt for me?" Margot asked. "I'll grab us coffees from Raine's booth."

"Sure." Garrett was happy to help.

"We've got it." Brandt watched his aunt walk away. "Thanks for helping. My aunt would do this herself if we weren't here. She's not old, but she shouldn't be climbing a stepladder by herself. And she's not a person to wait for her people to arrive."

"Not a problem."

Garrett shook the display rack to make sure it was steady. "This thing is solid."

"Aunt Margot had it made for this fair. It also fits in her front window for the Christmas contest."

Together, they hung the quilt.

He adjusted his side. "People here take their competitions seriously."

Brandt rolled his eyes. "When I was growing up, my mom was involved in the Silver Falls Christmas Home Tour. They stopped that after two homeowners got into a fight over who won."

Garrett shook his head. "Life in a small town."

"Yep."

He stepped in front of the booth to see if the quilt hung straight. "Looks good."

Brandt nodded. "So, you and Taryn?"

"Huh?"

"You're together."

Garrett flinched. Brandt spoke as if it were a done deal, too. "We're...friends."

Brandt grinned wryly. "Very friendly, based on how close you sat at dinner last night."

"It was crowded," Garrett blurted. He wasn't trying to hide anything. Other than a few kisses, nothing had happened. "I mean...Margot's house was packed."

He was reaching, and he didn't know why. Maybe because this time with Taryn was no different from in December. And he didn't want anyone to think the two of them might turn into a couple.

"Hey, it's not a big deal. Callie mentioned it to me this morning. She's happy because she likes Taryn and she loves you. The only thing better would be if you were interested in Anna."

Anna Kent was the dog groomer who worked with Callie

and would be his sister's maid of honor next weekend. "Both are nice. Taryn and I had fun working on her booth, but…"

It would never work.

"…nothing's changed since December." There. He'd said it. "She lives here. I don't."

"True, but Taryn seems…I don't know…happier this week, even with all the stress."

Garrett didn't want to take credit, but he stood taller, hoping he'd improved her mood. "The patio's open, and she finished the booth. Both must be a relief to her."

"If you and Taryn are just friends, let's see if she and Keaton hit it off. He's more on the quiet side and will be in town for a month, watching Rex while we're on our honeymoon."

Garrett's muscles tensed. His hands balled into fists. "You sound like your aunt."

Brandt's face reddened. "Well, I have a reason."

Better be a good one. "What?"

"A baker in the family, even as someone's girlfriend, would be awesome."

He had a point. Only if that baker wasn't Taryn. "Hate to tell you, but Margot has a woman in mind for my little brother."

Someone who better not be Taryn.

Garrett would have to make sure Margot didn't wave her matchmaking wand or shoot cupid's arrow or whatever she used to pair couples in Taryn's direction. She didn't need a relationship to distract her from the bakery. After she figured things out with Lawson's Bakery though…

His stomach churned.

*Stop.* Turning around the bakery and dealing with her father would take time. Besides, what Taryn did in the future wasn't Garrett's business. Still, that realization didn't make him feel any better.

Brandt sighed. "I told my aunt to stop matchmaking. Otherwise, someone will get hurt. I should have known she wouldn't listen."

"She gave me a reprieve during this visit, but I have a feeling Margot will be up to her old tricks during my next trip."

Brandt laughed. "My aunt's a force of nature. When she sets her mind on something, she's unstoppable, but I'll talk to her again. The heart is nothing to toy with, especially when it's someone else's."

"Good luck. And please convince your aunt to retire from matchmaking." If Brandt succeeded, Margot wouldn't set up Taryn with some random guy after Garrett left Silver Falls.

"I'll do my best." Brandt glanced at the Wags and Tails booth. "I want to check on Callie."

Margot stood across the aisle at the Tea Leaves and Coffee Bean's booth.

"I'll see if your aunt needs anything else." After that, Garrett would go to Taryn's booth. "Let me know if Callie needs anything."

As he walked toward the Summer-Cuppa-themed stall, Margot met him halfway. She handed him a small cup. "Courtesy of Raine and her baristas."

"Thanks." He took a sip. The hot liquid went down smoothly and the hint of vanilla appealed to his tastebuds. "How does the quilt look?"

"As good as yesterday." She beamed. "I appreciate you and Brandt hanging it."

"I'm meeting my brothers at your house. Text me if you need anything."

"Are you bringing them to the fair today?"

Garrett nodded. "They'll want to see Callie and see if she has a to-do list for them."

He hoped to spend time with Taryn. He glanced at her booth where she and two of her employees filled the table with desserts. Garrett couldn't wait.

TARYN PLACED SMALL plates with slices of pie and cake on a tiered server. The picnic cookies aka watermelon frosted sugar cookies had been such a hit she kept them as a sample today. She would use up the lemon bars before bringing out the brownies.

"Anything else, Boss?" Brecken asked.

"Keep Jayden in line at the bakery."

Brecken chuckled. "Always."

He lumbered off, all arms and legs.

Finley wouldn't arrive until today's festivities opened, but she didn't need help yet. Carl was on the schedule to take his place later and work until the fair closed. It would have been easier if she hadn't lost three employees to the other bakery, but she couldn't change the past. If that trio had worked at the Summit Ridge booth yesterday, none had stopped by to say hello.

*Don't think about it.*

Taryn refilled her apron pocket with coupons before checking everything again. Samples, napkins, forks—everything was where it should be.

She blew out a breath.

Now all she had to do was wow every person who visited, so they would go to the bakery after the fair. Easy-peasy.

She gulped.

"Looks even better than yesterday." Garrett sauntered to the table in a brown T-shirt and tan shorts. The casual style suited him, but she wanted to see him in a tuxedo. He wasn't the best man. That honor belonged to Sam Merrill, who worked at Wags and Tails. But Callie mentioned her three brothers being ushers.

She couldn't believe the wedding was only a week away. And Garrett would leave Silver Falls two days after that.

Taryn's throat tightened.

*Don't think about it.* Especially with him right here.

She pressed her shoulders back. "Thanks."

Garrett peered at the desserts. "No brownies?"

"Not until later."

"That will disappoint Brandt."

"He'll be here tomorrow. In fact, I'll tell people to return if they want one."

"Might work."

She placed her hands on her hips. "You've had my brownies. Of course, it'll work."

He grinned. "Did you make them?"

Taryn raised her chin. "It's my recipe."

"Do you think anyone using it would be able to replicate yours?"

She bit her lip. The question was harder to answer than she thought it would be.

"Not a simple answer," he said.

"No, because if someone followed the directions, they should come out the same. But that doesn't always happen."

"I've messed up many recipes. It doesn't matter how careful I am."

"Everyone has, including me," she admitted. "Sometimes it's the recipe's fault, but more often than not a person skips a step or changes something, not realizing it'll make a difference."

"That would probably be me."

"My grandmother showed me how to cook, and my grandpa taught me how to bake. They paid for my baking and pastry arts degree so I could take things to the next level, especially with cakes."

"A forward-thinking couple."

"They were." She missed them, but working in the bakery kept them close to her heart. "My dad wasn't happy I spent two years there and did an internship elsewhere, but he knew I'd return to Silver Falls, and I did."

A top restaurant had offered her a full-time job following her internship, but she'd turned it down without a second thought. Her grandparents had invested in her to bring new skills to Lawson's. She'd never once considered not returning.

"And I'm still here."

For how much longer remained to be seen.

*Nope. Not going there today.*

She forced a smile. "What are you up to?"

"Seeing if you need anything."

Taryn touched her chest. No heart melting. Except it might be a little too late. "You really are sweet."

He leaned closer.

As his warm breath caressed her neck, tingles trailed down her shoulder to her arm.

"I am," he whispered. "But people need to think I'm the egotistical attorney, not a nice guy."

She raised a brow. "So the shark in the courtroom is all an act?"

"An award-winning performance."

"Your secret's safe with me." She tried not to laugh and kept her voice low. "Promise."

All Taryn had to do was turn her head slightly, and she could kiss him. She wanted to, but did she dare with everyone she knew nearby, not to mention his sister and Margot at their booths or somewhere around here?

"Be sure to save me a portion of marionberry pie." Once again, his breath might as well be his hand. It caressed like a touch.

She swallowed a sigh. "I will."

Taryn would put a slice in the cooler for him.

"I hope I'm not late." The familiar voice meant an end to her time with Garrett. She drew away from him.

"You're not."

"Cool." Finley bounced into the booth like he was riding a pogo stick. Not unexpected. He was twenty and wore his long, blond hair in a man bun. He took classes at Summit Ridge University and worked at Lawson's as his schedule allowed. Right now, that meant full-time or split shifts because it was summer break. He put on an apron.

"I'm going to meet my brothers at Margot's and then come over here."

She'd glimpsed the other two Andrews brothers in December when they came into the bakery, but Garrett hadn't been with her then and they hadn't been introduced. Would he want her to meet them this time?

He studied Finley as if he were a specimen under a microscope before turning his attention on her. "Text if you need me to bring you lunch or anything."

Garrett was definitely a kindhearted lawyer. "Thanks, but I packed a lunch."

"See you soon."

He took two steps before glancing over his shoulder.

"Have fun with your family," she called out.

Garrett nodded, turned, and headed to Callie's booth.

Such a good big brother. Callie had mentioned her three siblings were overprotective. Still, knowing someone cared that much must be nice. Maybe someday Taryn would have in-laws, so she'd know what having a sibling was like.

"Welcome to the second day of the Silver Falls Summer Fair," a man announced over the speakers. "Be sure to check out the themed booths featuring our First Avenue businesses.

Silver Falls Flowers's Summer Blooms won first place last night, so be sure to congratulate them. The entertainment begins at eleven, and the carnival rides will open shortly. Have fun and don't forget to hydrate and wear sunscreen."

Finley smoothed his apron. "It's showtime."

"Put these in the front pocket." She handed him coupons. "Make sure every person gets one."

"Even the kids?"

"Not today, but tomorrow—they all need to go."

"Got it." Finley filled the pocket. "So, you and that lawyer guy are together again?"

"Again?"

"He always hung out at the bakery in December. And he'd wait for you to close up."

So much for no one noticing what she did. "He's helping me with the booth."

An edge of Finley's mouth slanted upward. "It's finished, yet he's still here."

How long would that last? He had no reason to spend time with her. Curl-her-toes kisses, aside. With his brothers in town, and the wedding next Saturday, he would be busy.

She shook her head. "Be sure to smile and hydrate. There's a cooler of water bottles and another with food if you get hungry."

Finley laughed. "Your non-answer is answer enough, Boss."

Taryn side-eyed him. "I am your boss, so you'd better watch it, or I'll give your goodie bag to Brecken."

❦

THE DAY PASSED by in a blur of telling people about the booth, handing out samples and coupons, and inviting them to visit the bakery. The temperature had to be in the nineties. A shower would refresh her and sitting down for a few hours would help her feet. They hurt from standing on the grass. Funny how she was more used to the tile floor at Lawson's. But it was worth a little discomfort to connect with so many potential customers.

A cute boy around four or five ran up to the booth. "Cookie, puh-lease."

A harried mom chasing after a toddler with sticky hands and face, glanced over her shoulder. "It's fine. He doesn't have any food allergies or intolerances."

Taryn handed him one. "Here you go."

He beamed. "Thanks." And he hurried to join his mom.

Nick came up to the table with a smug expression. At least he wore a button-down short-sleeve shirt with navy shorts and not a suit.

"Honorable mention." Nick reached up and flicked the ribbon tail. "Doubt that will bring you much exposure. Especially after we placed second."

"With my design."

"Summit Ridge Bakery did the work all themselves."

"Using my plans."

He clicked his tongue. "Don't be such a sore loser. It doesn't suit you, Taryn. You were never this whiney before, but I'll mention that when I meet with your father."

Her mouth dropped open. She closed it. "What did you say?"

Nick sneered. "Before your father's cruise, he set up an appointment with the owners of Summit Ridge Bakery to discuss the future of Lawson's Bakery. I owe you a big thank you for driving the value down these past months with your mismanagement of the place."

Her blood boiled. Her heart split open. She didn't want to believe her dad had done that without telling her. But that was another sign of how he saw her. And if Nick was being truthful, she would only hurt herself—and possibly Lawson's—if she spoke up.

Taryn motioned to the desserts on the table. "Would you like a slice?"

"No, thanks. I prefer the ones from Summit Ridge."

A man cleared his throat.

Nick glanced over his shoulder.

That gave her an unobstructed view of Garrett, flanked by two other men who resembled him. Must be his brothers.

"If you aren't interested in tasting Lawson's samples, move along." Garrett crossed his arms over his chest. His brothers did the same. "You're in the way."

Nick stiffened. "Uh…"

The Andrews men made an imposing wall. Taryn appreciated their efforts, but she didn't want to cause a scene. "He was just leaving."

Without a word, Nick scurried away like the rat he'd become.

She waited until he was out of earshot, and the three brothers stepped closer to the table. "Thank you."

"We're lovers, not fighters," the older one said. "But that

jerk doesn't know it."

The taller, thinner one with glasses nodded. "Brandt says Nick Baxter is all talk. He can't produce the results and cuts bait before he's found out."

"Taryn Lawson, I want you to meet my brothers."

She smiled at them "I hope your flight went well."

"It did." Keaton motioned to his oldest brother. "Except he almost killed us twice on the drive from Seattle."

Flynn rolled his eyes. "Time is money. And neither incident was that close."

"Close only counts in horseshoes and grenades," Garrett said.

Taryn laughed. "I see what Callie meant."

Flynn flashed a charming grin. "All good I'm sure."

Garrett elbowed him. "Stop flirting."

"The watermelon slices intrigue me." Keaton glanced from the cookies to her. "May I?"

"Of course. They are free." She handed him a coupon. "We have all our samples for sale in the bakery on First Avenue."

Garrett surveyed the table. "I hope you saved me a slice of marionberry pie."

She tried to act surprised. "Oh, was I supposed to?"

"Yes." He looked around the booth. "Where is it?"

Taryn almost laughed. "You have a one-track mind."

Flynn snickered. "She knows you well."

She nodded. "And you didn't say the magic words."

Garrett scratched his cheek. "À la mode."

Keaton shook his head. "That's three words."

"Oh, right." Garrett winked at her. "Please."

"Ignore Keaton or Garrett. They aren't worth your time." Flynn was model gorgeous with darker hair than his brother and lines at the corners of his eyes. "My lawyer brother told us your name, but I'm Doctor Flynn Andrews."

Keaton scoffed. "Notice how he says doctor. I could do that with my PhD, but I don't because it's pretentious. I'm happy to spell that, Dr. Flynn, if it's beyond your meager vocabulary."

Garrett rolled his eyes before mouthing "I'm sorry" to her.

Poor Callie. She must have had a hard time with how competitive her three older brothers were. Taryn removed her disposable glove and extended her arm to Flynn. "It's nice to meet you."

"It's a pleasure." Flynn raised her hand to his mouth and kissed it. "You're as sweet as the desserts you bake."

"Mine," Garrett growled.

Taryn bit back a laugh. She had no idea he was so possessive. But she kind of liked it.

Flynn side-eyed his brother. "Already?"

Garrett nodded once. "Should have arrived earlier, Doc."

"Don't mind my two older brothers." Keaton was cute with a geek-nerd vibe. "You're Callie's friend who's making the wedding cakes."

"You mean, cake, Professor," Flynn chided.

Keaton, who Callie called the brainy professor, was as attractive as Flynn, only not as handsome as Garrett. "Plural is correct. Your sister and Brandt ordered a three-tiered wedding cake and three groom cakes."

Flynn rubbed his neck before grabbing a lemon bar. "That's a lot of cake."

Garrett feigned annoyance while motioning to Flynn. "See what Callie and I dealt with growing up."

Taryn would play along. "I do. It must have been so difficult."

"Hey. No fair. Garrett got a head start, making an impression." Keaton took another cookie from a serving tray. "Give us time to catch up."

"Callie's in a class by herself and grew up fine." Flynn pointed to Garrett. "Now this guy... Trust me, Taryn, I put him to shame."

Taryn would trust the arrogant doctor—his sister's nickname for him—about as far as she could throw him. Which given his height and athletic build would be a few centimeters.

Garrett's face flushed. "Please ignore them. They act like they're twelve."

Flynn shook his head. "Thirteen."

"Eleven for me." Keaton tapped his chin with his free hand. "That would make Garrett twelve."

Taryn laughed, pulling on a new glove. "Margot will enjoy having you stay with her."

"She's got big plans in store." Garrett's tone was mysterious. "Why don't you guys look around? I'll catch up in a minute."

A man and his young daughter came up to the booth.

She pointed. "Slice of watermelon, please."

"They're cookies," the man explained.

"I know, but they're shaped like slices." She pointed to the Slice of Summer sign. "That's what I want, Daddy."

The man nodded.

Taryn handed the girl a watermelon cookie. "Enjoy your slice."

The girl clutched the cookie as if it were a special treasure. "I will. Thank you."

The dad peered at the sweets on the tiered tray. "I'll take a slice of pie. Any flavor."

Taryn grabbed the one nearest to her. "Here you go."

The girl took a bite. "Yum. This is better than real watermelon and way better than those cookies at the forest booth."

*Out of the mouth of babes.*

The praise ricocheted through Taryn, filling the empty spaces inside and making her stand taller.

She hoped other people did an impromptu test between the two bakeries and bought from Lawson's in the future. They might not get the exposure winning brought, but that would help. She wiggled her toes.

Garrett stared at her expectantly.

*Oh, right.*

*His pie.*

As the dad and daughter walked away, Taryn reached into the cooler and removed the slice she'd saved for Garrett. "One slice of marionberry pie for you."

He grinned. "Thanks."

Awareness hummed inside her. Suddenly, all was right in

her world. "You haven't tried the pie."

His gaze lingered on her. "I want the moment to last."

She laughed, more a show of nerves from the way he looked at her. It was as if he wanted a taste of her lips instead. She swallowed. "I can make more. All you have to do is ask."

# Chapter Fifteen

ON SUNDAY AFTERNOON, Taryn stood behind the table at her booth. Despite being tired and sweaty, she didn't want to be anywhere else. Lawson's couldn't make up the declining sales in three days, but this was the second weekend in a row business showed improvement. A good—and much-needed—sign. The booth's traffic exceeded last summer's traffic. She would figure out the profit made tomorrow. Tonight, a shower and sleep were her only priorities. She also hoped the coupons brought more customers into the bakery.

Most of the people were snagging desserts off the table without stopping to chat.

She didn't mind. The drive-by—okay, walk-by—visits always happened toward the end of the fair.

The pile of coupons had dwindled to a handful, so Jayden had estimated well.

Now, all she needed was to see Garrett.

Strike that.

Taryn didn't need to see him. She wanted to see him.

Semantics, yes, but a big difference in her mind.

He'd stopped by briefly this morning to ask if she needed

help, but Taryn had everything under control. That didn't stop her from waiting for him to show up again.

That was silly.

He must be with his family like last night when he'd had dinner with them and Brandt's parents and aunt. Taryn hadn't been invited to join them nor had she expected to be. The whole reason he was in Silver Falls was to be with his family. She assumed the same thing would happen tonight and every night this week.

That didn't make her want to see Garrett less.

Not silly.

Pathetic.

"Only thirty minutes until the summer fair closes," a voice announced. "This is your last chance to visit the fabulous First Avenue booths and use your ride tickets."

Anna worked in the Wags and Tails booth with her little dog, Milo, who posed as if he were a part of the decorations. That was better than him causing trouble, as he was known to do. Anna wasn't packing up yet, but she'd made piles of items to ease cleanup. Raine appeared to be doing the same thing.

Taryn didn't blame them. Both women need to be at work early in the morning. So did she, yet she would wait for any last visitors. Not that a handful of customers would make a difference, but she wanted them to feel as welcome as those who'd stopped by on Friday. Each person counted.

Garrett approached. "Things are slowing down."

Her pulse skittered. "Yes. People are likely over at the rides trying to get the most out of their unlimited ride bracelets or tickets."

"Lots are over at the bakery."

Excitement shot through her. "Wonderful."

"Yes." She glanced in at the other booths on either side of her. "That must be why Brecken isn't here yet."

"How do you feel about how things went?"

"I'm thrilled, so is Jayden. He texted me that business is up, and not every customer redeemed the coupons we've been giving away."

"That's great."

She nodded. "I won't have the exact numbers until tomorrow, but I feel good about it. We don't have the staff to support opening on Sundays, but it might be worth trying one or two days a month as an experiment."

"As long as you take off another day. You don't want to burn out."

His kind tone didn't hide how amusing she found his words. "Says the workaholic attorney."

He sheepishly grinned as if caught taking the last cookie.

Talk about adorable.

"I should do the same," he admitted.

"You should." Taryn couldn't hold back the laughter. "We're a pair."

"Yes, we are." He sounded amused. "In our defense, we enjoy what we do for a living. There's no crime in that."

She nodded. "What's that adage...when you love your job it doesn't feel like work?"

"I've heard that, but it's still a lot of work for me."

"True." Her gaze traveled from each of the desserts remaining on the table. Pride swelled in her. "But I wouldn't want to do anything else."

Taryn hoped her dad gave her the chance to keep running Lawson's in some capacity.

Garrett reached out, held her hand, and squeezed. "It'll all work out."

How did he read her so well? Before she could reply, Brecken ran up to the booth. Reluctantly, she pulled her hand away.

Brecken's cheeks were flushed, and he still wore a hairnet and his bakery whites. "Jayden sent me over to help you pack up."

"We have a few more minutes left," she said.

"Cool." His breath came fast. He must have run. "Lots of people are in the shop."

"Wonderful." Taryn would discuss staying open on an occasional Sunday with Jayden, and then they could talk to the others. She would need at least three of their staff willing to commit to an extra day.

"What should I do?" Brecken asked.

She pointed to the plastic containers they'd brought baked goods over in. "Leave a couple of those out, but put the rest into the cardboard boxes, please."

"Sure thing, Boss." He wiped his hands on his apron and stacked them. "Now that they're empty, they'll be easier to carry. Want me to take these to the bakery?"

"That would be great, but don't carry too many. I don't want you to trip."

"I'll be careful." A minute or two later, he held on to a

large box. "Be right back."

The lanky teen hurried away.

Garrett watched him go. "Tell me about Brecken."

"He's a sweet kid. He started working at the bakery two years ago to save for community college and help his family. His siblings cut the coupons."

Garrett lowered his gaze to the table, staring at the plate of brownies as if it contained the winning numbers for the upcoming lottery drawing. That was odd.

"Why do you want to know about Brecken?" She waited for an answer, but he remained silent. "Garrett?"

"I'm good at figuring out people. It's a useful skill with selecting juries."

"Okay." Except it wasn't if he used that with her or her employees. "What does this have to do with Brecken?"

"He's wearing three-hundred-dollar tennis shoes."

The words sunk in. She immediately rejected what he implied. "No."

"Taryn—"

"No." The word flew out. She shook her head as if to emphasize the point. "Brecken is the oldest of seven children. His family lives in an apartment and can barely afford rent because his dad was in a terrible accident and on disability. Brecken's mom works two jobs. They must be knockoffs."

"He has the motivation."

Her stomach went rock hard. "You think Brecken stole…"

She couldn't finish the sentence.

A guy ran up and grabbed a brownie from the table.

"Love these."

Garrett handed him a coupon. "They're available every day at Lawson's Bakery on First Avenue."

His voice was firmer than usual. The tension from earlier in the week was back, and she hated that when things had gotten so comfortable between them. She bit her lip.

The man picked up another brownie before walking away.

"Hear me out before you say anything else," Garrett said before she could tell him he was out of his mind for accusing Brecken of this.

She took a breath. "Go ahead."

"If his family is struggling that much, he has reason to sell your recipes and designs."

Taryn shook her head. "I understand what you're saying, but it makes no sense. Why would he buy expensive shoes instead of putting aside money for rent and groceries? Unless they were gifts."

Garrett nodded. "That would make things less traceable to whoever gave them."

Nick Baxter was implied.

Taryn wrapped her arms around herself. It didn't take away the sick feeling in her stomach.

"I can't believe it…" Her heart ached. Brecken loved the bakery and wouldn't hurt it or Taryn. "He's a sweet kid, who likes to make jokes, and he's never late for work or missed a shift. He wouldn't steal from Lawson's."

Garrett's jaw tensed. "You only know what you've seen or been told. You can't look behind a door or into someone's heart."

That was true.

"All we have to do is talk to him and listen to how he answers."

"You're the experienced one with this, but I still don't like it, and you'll see you're wrong."

"I hope I am."

She studied him. "You sound as if you mean that."

"I do," Garrett admitted. "I would rather find out Baxter paid someone to break into Lawson's and steal things."

An unpleasant, violated sensation crawled along her spine. "I suppose that would be better."

But not by much. She shivered.

"The Silver Falls Summer Fair is now closed," a woman announced over the loudspeakers. "Thanks for attending. Don't forget to shop locally at the First Avenue shops. We'll see you next year."

Garrett rubbed his hands together. "Let's clean up."

"What about your brothers?"

"They headed over to Callie's place to do a few things for the wedding."

She packed the remaining dessert samples and the leftover coupons. They would recycle those.

Garrett cut the zip ties holding decorations in place on the pop-up tent, and she packed them into boxes. She folded the canopy's top while he removed the tree trunks from the front poles. Together, they collapsed the tent's frame.

"Wow." Openmouthed, Brecken approached, staring at them. "You guys are fast."

"Takedown is always faster." Garret motioned to the tent. "Do you mind putting that in its case?"

"Happy to do it." As Brecken bent over, something dropped onto the ground.

Garrett picked up a cell phone and handed it over. "Is this the newest model?"

"Yeah." Brecken put it in his pocket. "Mr. Baxter accidentally dropped my old one in the lake when he took me and his kids fishing, so he bought it for me."

Garrett shot her an I-told-you-so look. "Nick Baxter?"

Brecken nodded. "I babysit his kids. Before he drives me home, he lets me play his PS4. That system is fire. My old Xbox broke, so I don't play games much."

Garrett nodded. "That sure is nice of him."

"Yeah, he's an all-right guy." Brecken held out his foot. "He got me these shoes when he noticed the holes in my other ones. I've never had a brand-new pair before. Pretty cool, huh?"

*No, no, no.* Taryn clutched a tree bark so hard her fingernails dug into the foam.

"Did Nick ever ask you to do something in return for the things he gave you?" Garrett folded the picnic tablecloth.

"He hasn't been sketchy or creepy, if that's what you're worried about. I mean, Mr. Baxter hates Brandt Winslow, who's always been nice to me. But Mr. Baxter thought Brandt and Callie should have ordered their wedding cake from Summit Ridge, not us, which I don't understand because Mr. Baxter only consults with that bakery. He doesn't own it."

She hadn't been sure of Nick's involvement, but that made more sense given he was more of a tech guy—well, the business side of things—and had no background in retail or food.

"But he's legit," Brecken added.

Garrett came closer. "Legit, how?"

Brecken looked at Taryn. "Remember how you and Jayden dictate recipes into my phone, so my dyslexia doesn't mess up me reading the directions?"

She nodded. "I'm sorry, we've been so busy and haven't done any of the newer ones."

"That's okay because Mr. Baxter offered. He didn't want me to bug you when you're so busy with the patio and adding items to the menu."

Garrett leaned closer to the teenager. "How did he help you?"

"I sent him a copy of the recipe, and he sent me recordings." Brecken sounded so proud. "Pretty sweet, and I saved everyone all that time. Mr. Baxter called it a win-win."

Taryn covered her mouth to keep from groaning. Brecken had no clue what he'd done. And in his defense, as Garrett would say, she'd never told Brecken not to share the recipes. Of course, she'd assumed the teenager would know not to do that.

She sighed.

Garrett's face hardened. "Nick Baxter sounds like a real stand-up guy."

Brecken nodded. "Mr. Baxter is. He always asks how Lawson's is doing. Even though he works with the other bakery, he legit wants to help because Mr. Baxter grew up with Taryn, which is why he asked about our booth. He wanted the two bakeries to work together at the fair to help ours. Then you changed themes, but they stuck with it."

Brecken might have graduated high school, but he was only eighteen. He'd led a sheltered life in the bubble known as Silver Falls. His family struggled financially, and Nick had used his wealth to take advantage of him. Flashing fancy items in front of a kid who'd lived in poverty his entire life was an abuse of power and circumstance.

She took a breath. "I need to tell you something."

"What?" Brecken asked with the eagerness of a puppy.

So curious. So young. So naïve.

A vise clamped around her heart and tightened. "I don't want to upset you, but you need to know…"

The teen's face fell. "Are you okay? Or is it your mom and dad? Did something happen on their vacation?"

His concern was one hundred percent sincere, which made this more challenging.

Garrett touched her shoulder.

The simple gesture gave her strength. She took another breath.

"My parents are fine, but Nick Baxter never discussed working with us at the summer fair. I didn't know they were using our design until Wednesday night, which is why I changed our theme." Taryn kept her voice steady, but her insides shook, twisting and turning over how badly the guy had used Brecken. "Nick isn't out to help us. He wants to destroy Lawson's Bakery and has been trying to take our

189

business away."

"But he's a good guy." Brecken raised his right foot. "I told you he got me these shoes."

She glanced at Garrett and mouthed *help*.

"He did, and they are cool shoes," Garrett agreed. "But he was trying to get on your good side."

"My good side?"

"He was using you."

Brecken shook his head. "He was helping us. Who would drop a phone into a lake on purpose? Sure, it was old, but it worked fine. I didn't need a fancy new one."

He sounded confused. Taryn didn't blame him. She found it hard to believe Nick would do this. And based on what he'd said the other night and what Brecken had told her, the vendetta had more to do with Brandt than Lawson's Bakery.

She needed to tell him the rest of what had happened. "Whatever Nick might have told you, he gave the recipes he recorded to Summit Ridge Bakery. They are selling our products, cutting the prices, and taking away our customers."

Brecken's forehead creased. "But Nick said he wants to help us."

"He lied to you."

Brecken tilted his head before opening his mouth. "He wasn't trying to help?"

"No," Taryn said softly. "He wanted to hurt us."

Garrett nodded. "Nick didn't talk to Taryn, nor did Summit Ridge. They took the designs you shared with Nick and claimed them as their own."

Brecken inhaled sharply. "No one like him ever gave my family or me the time of day. I thought... I thought Mr. Baxter was my friend, but he...wasn't."

"No, he wasn't."

Brecken hung his head. "All the trouble the bakery has been having with fewer customers coming in. It's my fault."

"Hey." Taryn reached out and touched Brecken's hand. "You didn't know."

"I didn't." Brecken's eyes gleamed. "I really didn't. I thought he was legit a good guy. He bought me fancy stuff. Paid twenty bucks an hour for the babysitting so that I could help my family more." Brecken sniffled. "I love working at Lawson's and baking. I'm finally good at something. And you and Jayden always send me home with extra for my family. More than you give Carl and Finley."

Seeing Brecken so upset hurt Taryn's heart. She patted his hand. "I don't blame you. Nick's the one at fault."

"You trusted someone who took advantage of you." Garrett's deep voice must resonate in a courtroom. "He used you, but now that Taryn knows how Summit Ridge got hold of the recipes and designs, it'll stop."

Brecken glanced up before his face crumpled. Tears fell. "What if it's too late?"

"I'm not giving up." She only hoped her father gave her the chance to turn things around. "No one at Lawson's is. That includes you."

Brecken groaned again. "This is like real-life spy stuff. I can't go to jail. I'm supposed to start community college in the fall, and I would never hurt..."

"I know you wouldn't." Taryn didn't hesitate to answer.

"No one is going to jail," Garrett said in a matter-of-fact tone. "We just need to figure out what to do next."

"And we will," Taryn assured Brecken. "It'll be okay."

"But it's not okay now. And it might not be okay. I ruined everything." Brecken wiped his face with his arm. "I should have known it was too good to be true. Are you firing me?"

"No." Taryn didn't hesitate to answer. Brecken was a hardworking employee. He might have been naïve, but his reaction told her he wouldn't do this again. "Lawson's needs you."

More tears fell. "Even after what I did?"

She nodded.

Brecken glanced at Garrett. "You're a lawyer, right?"

Garrett nodded.

"Are you sure they won't arrest me for corporate spying or something?"

"I'm sure," he replied.

"You're safe," she said firmly. "Nothing will happen to you. But I wish Nick would have to pay for what he's done."

"I'm sorry, Taryn." Brecken's shoulders shook. "So, so sorry."

She tried to comfort him. "I know you are."

"Everyone makes mistakes." Empathy oozed from Garrett in waves. "I did when I was in college. All you can do is learn your lesson and move on from there."

"My dad tells me that, but he also taught me to take responsibility for my mistakes. I need this job badly. My family can't cover the rent without my paycheck, and I want you to trust me again." His voice trembled. "I'll fix this, Boss. I'll make it better. I promise."

Brecken took off running through the park in the opposite direction of First Avenue.

Taryn wiped her eyes. "It's not his fault."

Garrett blew out a breath. "I know."

She had to make this right. "What do we do now?"

# Chapter Sixteen

S UNDAY NIGHT, NO one had heard from Brecken. Garrett sat in the bakery that was now closed. The staff cleaned up in the kitchen while Taryn spoke to Brecken's mother on the phone.

Garrett hated the toll this was taking on Taryn. Worry etched into lines on her forehead and around her mouth. She kept moving as if stopping would mean something terrible would happen. The nervous energy had intensified the past two hours.

His family, Brandt's family, and Callie's and Margot's employees were searching Silver Falls both in their cars and on foot for the missing teen. Not everyone had met Brecken, but a tall kid dressed in his white uniform shouldn't be hard to spot.

But so far, no one had seen him.

Not good.

Garrett dragged his hand through his hair.

Taryn continued to pace in front of the display case. "Okay, thanks… I appreciate that, and I'll do the same… Talk to you soon. Bye."

She disconnected from the call, lowered her phone, and

slumped.

He stood. Jayden, Carl, and Finley came out of the kitchen. All three had changed out of their uniforms and wore shorts and T-shirts.

"Any word?" Jayden's worry was apparent in those two words.

"None. His family has been reaching out to his friends, but no one has talked to Brecken." Taryn rubbed her eyes. "It's as if he's disappeared. He wants to fix this, but I have no idea what he meant by that. Neither do his parents. I hope he's okay."

Jayden hugged her.

That should be Garrett's job, but he was the outsider here. These people had worked with Brecken for two years and cared about him. While Garrett had seen him around the bakery, he'd only met the teenager today.

"Someone will find him." Jayden raised Taryn's chin with his finger. "I spoke to Rachelle. She's getting the word out to first responders in Silver Falls and the surrounding areas. People are out looking for him."

"Brecken's a good kid," Carl said. "He can get tunnel vision, whether that's icing cupcakes or fixing what he did wrong. And he won't come up for air until he's finished."

"That's Brecken all right." Finley's smile, however, was fleeting. "I've been texting him, but he hasn't replied. I'm guessing his phone is blowing up with people trying to contact him. His phone might be dead."

"A dead battery would explain why no one can reach him." Garrett was grasping at straws and not handling the situation with his usual calmness and emotional distance. He much preferred being on the sidelines. "We'll find him."

"We will." But her tone lacked confidence. "There's no reason for us to stay here. I'm sure if Brecken shows up anywhere, it'll be his house. You've all worked so hard this weekend, and tomorrow's another workday, so why doesn't everyone go home? If anyone hears anything, let everybody know."

"Good plan," Jayden agreed. "And thanks for all the extra time you guys put in today."

Taryn nodded. "We couldn't have pulled off the summer fair without you, so thank you."

Finley and Carl muttered *you're welcome.*

Jayden pinned Garrett with a hard stare. "You staying with her?"

"I am."

"Good." Jayden hugged her again as if to get under Garrett's skin—it was working. "Hang in there."

She stared at the floor. "If I hadn't mentioned Nick to him—"

"This isn't your fault," Garrett interrupted.

Taryn opened her mouth.

"Listen to the lawyer." Jayden glanced his way. "He's right for once."

Garrett cocked a brow. "For once?"

Jayden's jaw jutted forward, but amusement shone in his eyes. "You've scored a few points, but you need to earn more, attorney guy."

Carl snickered.

Finley laughed.

Taryn rolled her eyes. "And with that, good night all. See you tomorrow."

"See ya, Boss." Finley headed to the door.

Carl followed. "In the morning, we'll give Brecken a hard time and make him clean the bathroom."

"Call me if you need anything," Jayden said to Taryn before shooting him a take-care-of-her look.

Garrett intended to do that.

The door to the bakery opened, and the familiar ping filled the air. The three men left, and the sound repeated when the door closed.

He was more of an overprotective big brother, but he'd had a few high-maintenance clients, so caretaking wasn't entirely outside his wheelhouse. "Let's get something to eat."

"You should be with your family."

"They are looking for Brecken. And before you tell me you want to join in the search, that's not happening." He stepped toward her. "You've worked hard all weekend and need to rest."

"But—"

Garrett silenced her with a kiss. He waited for her to pull away, but she pressed harder against his lips. As he soaked up the taste of her, he relished the feel of her.

He'd wanted to kiss her—hold her—since the other night, but the timing hadn't been right with the fair. This might not be a perfect time, either, but they were together and alone. That was enough.

Garrett wrapped his arms around Taryn and pulled her

even closer. He kissed her as if he'd never get the chance again, running his fingers through her hair.

*Ding.*

She stiffened before pulling away.

That was when he realized they weren't alone.

"Brecken!" she yelled.

Garrett glanced at the door to see Brecken with Flynn and Keaton. Only yellow feathers were missing from his brothers' canary-eating grins.

Taryn rushed toward the teenager and hugged him. "Are you okay?"

Brecken blushed. "I didn't mean to make people worry."

"Did you get in touch with your mom and dad?" she asked.

Garrett glanced at Flynn and Keaton. "Yeah."

Something was going on, and it involved his brothers. He gave both his spill-now look.

"He used my phone," Keaton said, not offering much.

Garrett prepared to go into cross-examination mode.

"Dial it back, Gar," Flynn said. "Some kid mentioned seeing Brecken at the Summit Ridge Bakery, so we drove over there."

"How did you get to Summit Ridge?" Taryn asked.

"I walked," Brecken answered as if that would have only taken him ten minutes when it would have been an hour or two, depending on his pace. "I thought about hitching a ride, but my parents told me never to do that."

"Never do that," all three brothers said in unison.

Taryn appeared confused.

So was Garrett. "Can you start at the beginning?"

"Brecken?" she asked.

He inhaled deeply. "I told you I would fix things."

"You did," Taryn said.

"The only way for me to do that was to go to Summit Ridge, so I walked. I found a pawnshop. Did you know they're open on Sundays?"

"No," she said. "Go on."

"Oh, well, first I headed to the drugstore and bought a pair of flip-flops and a bottle of water. I was sweating, and my mom always says to hydrate. Anyway, after that, I headed over to the Summit Ridge Bakery where I filmed videos of me telling what they did and put them online."

"Not on one platform," Keaton clarified. "Everywhere."

"He made posts, too," Flynn added. "With receipts from his emails with Nick Baxter."

Brecken nodded. "Gotta keep the receipts."

"Yes, you do." Garrett didn't like what had happened, but the kid's actions to "fix things" impressed him. "What did you do after that?"

"I sold my phone and shoes at the pawnshop."

"That's why he needed the flip-flops," Keaton, always the professor and filling in gaps, added.

"No shoes, no service." Brecken pointed to the small sign on the bakery's door. "Plus, walking home barefoot might have hurt."

Garrett glanced at Brecken's feet. Canvas sneakers had replaced the expensive pair he wore earlier. "Why did you sell your things?"

"I didn't want them. Not knowing why Mr. Baxter gave them to me." Brecken shuddered before pulling money from his pocket and handing it to Taryn. "This is from the pawnshop. I want Lawson's to have it."

She stared at the bills. "I don't understand."

He rubbed his hands on his white pants. "It's not nearly as much as the bakery has lost because of what I gave Nick, but it's all I have."

Taryn's eyes gleamed. "Thank you, but you need a cell phone and real shoes."

Brecken's grin brightened his face. "Keaton and Flynn took care of that. They each bought me shoes. Oh, and Flynn got me a phone."

Keaton's cheeks reddened. "It was the least we could do. A guy needs more than one pair of shoes, especially if he's starting college in the fall."

Flynn's chest puffed. "And a cell phone."

"I told them I didn't need them." Brecken shrugged. "But they insisted."

"Of course, they did." Pride over his brothers' actions flowed through Garrett. He also saw what Taryn had meant about Brecken being a sweet kid. "As they should have."

"Thank you." She hugged Flynn and then Keaton. "For finding Brecken, buying him those things, and driving him to Silver Falls."

A part of the story was missing. Garrett looked at Keaton. "How did you know where to find him?"

"I teach kids his age," Keaton said in a matter-of-fact tone. "So we asked teenagers in town, and one mentioned seeing his video from the Summit Ridge Bakery."

Brecken grinned. "It went viral."

Flynn laughed. "I have a feeling that other bakery will spend all their profits on a PR person to put out the fires Brecken set on every social media platform."

Brecken stood taller. "Told you I'd fix it."

"You did. And I appreciate it." Taryn smiled softly. "But you scared many people who care about you when you took off. Try to remember to tell someone where you're going the next time, okay?"

He nodded. "My mom and dad were so happy when I called I don't think I'll be in that much trouble."

Garrett forced himself to laugh. "That's good, but just because you get away with something once doesn't mean you do it again."

"That's right," Keaton agreed. "Otherwise, you'll end up needing to hire an overpriced attorney like my brother."

Everyone laughed.

"We'll take Brecken home and explain things to his parents," Keaton said.

"You've both had a long day." Flynn gave Taryn a once-over that made Garrett scoot closer to her. "Get food and then rest. Doctor's orders."

Keaton groaned. "There he goes with the doctor title again."

"Come on, little brother." Flynn opened the door, and the familiar ding sounded. "Let's take Brecken home so these two can go back to what they were doing when we arrived."

It was Taryn's turn to blush.

Brecken snickered.

Keaton grinned. "Carry on, friends."

Seriously? Garrett shook his head.

They walked out, and the door closed behind them. The ding rang again.

"I'm sorry for Keaton and Flynn."

Taryn typed on her phone. "You don't have to apologize. I'll send them a box of desserts tomorrow for what they did. I need to tell the others Brecken is safe."

"You were right about the kid."

Her grin, complete with dimples, lit up her beautiful face. "Told you so."

"You did. And to make up for it, dinner is on me."

"Sounds good." She tucked away her phone, added the cash to a drawer beneath the counter, and locked it. "I want to go home, though. How does Chinese takeout sound?"

He was happy to do whatever she wanted. "Perfect."

And it was. Tonight hadn't turned out like any of them had planned, but it would end well.

ON MONDAY, TARYN arrived at the bakery while the sky was still dark and the sun fast asleep. She'd taken Jayden's shift so he could spend the day with his wife, who was off. Taryn yawned, even after sleeping several hours. She'd fallen asleep on Garrett's shoulder after they ate last night, so he'd woken her, told her to go to bed, and kissed her forehead. And she had.

She pulled the tray of muffins out of the oven and slid in

another.

The only problem?

Well, two problems.

He'd mentioned this week would be busy, and his free time would be scarce.

Translation number one: I probably won't see you until the wedding.

And second, he would leave a week from today.

Translation number two: the fact she considered this a problem should concern her.

*We're friends hanging out, sharing hot kisses.*

And if her heart bumped when she saw him or thought of him, that was because of the newness of everything. It meant nothing.

They would have to make the most of whatever time they had together before they said goodbye.

No big deal.

Maybe if she kept telling herself that, she would believe it.

She grabbed a cranberry scone off the cooling rack and bit into it.

Though probably not.

The bakery's landline rang.

Strange. The sun wasn't up. Who would call this early?

It might be Carl, Finley, or Brecken, so she'd better answer. "Lawson's Bakery. This is Taryn. How can I help you?"

"Good morning, Taryn."

She clutched the phone. "Dad? Is everything okay?"

"I should ask you that. I saw Brecken's videos and posts.

Is it true?"

"Yes." She pressed her lips together to keep from saying I told you so.

"I don't know what to say."

Taryn had to say it. "You might reconsider your meeting with them."

Silence filled the line.

"You know about that?"

His tone didn't tell her much, but his words were slower. "Nick Baxter mentioned it yesterday."

"He's no longer associated with the Summit Ridge Bakery."

"I hadn't heard that." Of course not. It was four thirty in the morning. "How do you know that?"

"The owners emailed me last night."

O-kay. "Does that mean you're still meeting with them?"

"Your mother and I want you to have a life."

"I have a life. One I enjoy very much."

"All you do is work at the bakery."

"I love baking."

"It's too much for you. You should date more so you can fall in love, get married, and have children."

Huh? He made no sense. "I'm doing what you did."

"That was different."

Taryn had a feeling as to the reason, but she needed him to say. "How?"

He said nothing.

"Dad, what's different?"

"I had your mother to raise you and take care of the

house and all the other stuff that goes along with having a child. No man wants his wife working the hours you do. You've done a good job with the bakery, but your mother and I discussed this, and we're selling it. If you want to keep working there, you can until—"

"Until I meet a man." The words tasted like a burnt cookie.

"Yes. It's the best thing for you."

As if she were a child and not a thirty-two-year-old woman. And it wasn't as if her parents were that old. Her mother might not have had a career outside of the house, but many others did. "It's not. I can do both."

"That's what people say, but it's not true. If you'd married before I retired, this would have been much easier for you to understand."

The truth smacked Taryn in the head like a loaf of bread that had been underproofed or over-kneaded. Her father's criticisms over her wanting to update the menu and remodel made sense now. He hadn't wanted her to make any changes because Lawson's Bakery wouldn't be hers.

"You never planned to turn the bakery over to me." The words came out calmer than she expected.

"No, we didn't."

Her breath hitched. "Did Grandpa know?"

"Yes, and he and your grandmother disagreed with us. But my mother always considered herself progressive and a feminist. That's why they paid for you to go to the culinary academy."

"So I'd have a backup." Taryn startled, realizing she'd

said the words aloud. Tears stung her eyes. "When were you going to tell me?"

More silence.

"I've poured myself into the bakery. I deserve an answer," she pressed.

"After I signed the contract."

When there was nothing she could do. Not that she could do anything now that she knew the information.

She swallowed around the lump in her throat. "It's a done deal?"

"Not quite."

But *almost* was implied.

Her heart sank like a cake does when someone opened the oven door too often. She had to say something before he destroyed her grandparents' legacy. "You might want to reconsider selling to the owners of Summit Ridge, given their sketchy behavior."

"Your mother and I will discuss it when I return. There's no rush."

Not for them.

What about her?

Taryn glanced around the bakery. This place was where she'd grown up. It was supposed to be her future. She still wanted it to be. That gave her an idea.

She took a breath. "Forget about the Summit Ridge folks. Sell Lawson's to me."

# Chapter Seventeen

THE WEEK PASSED by in a blur for Taryn. Summit Ridge Bakery had issued a public apology. They'd mentioned cutting ties with their consultant, Nick Baxter. Lawson's business was up to holiday levels thanks to the coupons and people wanting to support them after hearing what had happened. With the increased traffic, she'd hired Brecken's oldest sister, Mandy, who was sixteen and wanting a part-time job to save money for college.

Taryn's parents hadn't called, but that didn't stop her from applying for a small business loan. She wanted to buy Lawson's. If they decided not to sell it to her, she would open a place of her own. The decision wasn't out of spite or for revenge. Taryn was a baker and owning a bakery was her dream. She would make it happen. Somehow.

It was as simple as that.

How complicated things became remained to be seen.

Not that she'd told anyone, including her employees.

Anything she said would be premature. The sale to the Summit Ridge Bakery owners might not happen. However, she'd been tempted to tell Garrett. Except that wasn't something you said to a friend who was leaving on Sunday.

So, she'd kept quiet.

Despite helping Callie with wedding stuff, he'd had coffee with her on Monday and Wednesday. They'd also eaten lunch at the Falls Café on Tuesday. She'd missed seeing him yesterday, but there'd been a play-golf-pseudo-bachelor-party for the guys. Taryn, however, would see him at the rehearsal dinner, if only for a few minutes, but she'd take it. She parked behind a car in Margot's driveway. She unloaded the first box of desserts from the trunk, carried them to the front of the house, and rang the bell.

Margot opened the door. "Come in out of that heat."

"Thanks." Taryn stepped inside. "At least it's only in the eighties."

"Very true. I had a special tent set up for the dessert bar."

"I can't wait to see it, but I have more I need to get. The other desserts are in coolers, so they don't melt."

"Pippa is still decorating and hanging fairy lights and tulle. She shouldn't be much longer." Margot glanced at the clock as if to confirm her plans. "Let's put these in the fridge while you bring in the others."

It took Taryn three more trips. "This is the last one."

"Pippa's gone, and the caterers are setting up."

Taryn climbed the short staircase to the backyard that Pippa transformed into a romantic hideaway with white tulle and fairy lights. Globe bulbs hung along the edge of the cover and crisscrossed the width. With the large tent and two smaller ones—for the bar and dessert buffet—blocking the direct sunlight, the temperature was cooler. She noticed an outdoor air conditioner. Margot had gone all out for her nephew.

"This is lovely." A wooden table with serving stands of various heights. "Has Callie seen this yet?"

"No, and neither has Brandt."

"They'll love it." The decked-out backyard was as elegant as any wedding venue. "I'll get set up."

With gloves on, Taryn arranged each of the desserts. She'd known Margot wanted a cake even though the bride and groom hadn't, so she'd made a strawberry shortcake as a surprise for the quilt shop owner. And the angel food cake with strawberries and whipped cream was the perfect centerpiece for the buffet. As she stored the cooler, the scent of the delicious dinner tickled her nose.

She removed her gloves and looked around. Beautiful. And not only the desserts.

Taryn headed into the house where Margot was feeding her two dogs. "Everything's ready. If you run low on anything, there are extras in the coolers beneath the dinner buffet."

"Perfect."

The doorbell rang, and people quickly spilled into the backyard. Within minutes, music played, and the bartender poured drinks.

That was Taryn's cue to leave. "I'll pick up my things when it's convenient for you."

"Stay and eat before you leave."

Taryn hesitated. "I need to frost the wedding cakes."

Margot waved her off. "Fifteen minutes is nothing. Besides, it's dinnertime. You must be hungry."

When she put it that way... "Okay, but I can't stay long."

Taryn followed Margot outside, where people were eating dinner. That was quick. There had to be at least thirty guests. She knew some, like Anna and Raine, but not the others.

"Get a plate and make yourself at home." With that, Margot headed toward Brandt's mother.

As Taryn stood in the buffet line, she glimpsed Garrett talking to someone she didn't recognize.

A few minutes later, she sat at one of the round tables, listening to Margot tell the story of when Callie came over to make Christmas cookies. "I knew she belonged with Brandt, which proves once again that my matchmaking skills are second to none."

People laughed.

Funnily enough, or maybe not, neither Callie nor Brant denied it.

As the dinner progressed, Taryn felt like an interloper. She stayed off to the side, as far away from the center as she could. She noticed how Garrett and his brothers knew how to entertain a crowd. Then again, all three lived in Los Angeles. They must be used to parties and entertaining, given their professions.

After eating, she replenished the dessert bar before saying her goodbyes to Margot, Mr. and Mrs. Winslow, Brandt, and Callie.

As Taryn headed to the door, Garrett jogged up to her. "Where are you going?"

"To the bakery." She had brought only her keys, cell, and the desserts, so she could make a quick exit. "Your sister's wedding cakes won't frost themselves."

"I'll go with you," he said, as if he were discussing whether or not to press the crosswalk button.

"That's unnecessary. I drove."

"It's getting late."

"Nothing bad happens in Silver Falls. And the bakery is still open."

"Let's just say my escorting you there is insurance against anything happening to you before my little sister's big day."

"Fine," Taryn relented because she needed to get going. "But you're wasting precious time you could spend partying."

"There will be plenty of that tomorrow."

"Don't rush back," Margot called as if she'd been eavesdropping. "And thank you for the divine strawberry shortcake surprise."

Where had she come from? Taryn leaned closer to him and whispered, "She's not playing matchmaker, is she?"

"I told her not to."

"That's never stopped her in the past."

A thoughtful expression formed on his face. "This time, I believe her."

Taryn hoped he was right, or Margot would be disappointed.

Three nights from now, Garrett would be in California, which seemed as far away as Mars at the moment.

As they walked through Margot's house, he laced his fingers with hers. "The dessert buffet was the highlight."

"Thanks, but I don't think you can single anything out. From the decorations to the food, it was the nicest rehearsal dinner I've seen."

"The desserts were my favorite."

His compliment filled her with warmth. "Are you ready for tomorrow?"

"Not much the bride's brother needs to do other than drink at the reception and make a funny speech if asked. I've got both covered."

"Good, because Callie looks ready to burst with excitement." Taryn unlocked her car. "I think she'd get married tonight if it were possible."

"I disagree."

"Seriously?"

He nodded, mischief gleaming in his eyes.

She slid behind the steering wheel. "They had everything they needed."

Garrett sat in the passenger seat. "Not the wedding cake and three groom's cakes."

"Oh, I didn't think about those." Which surprised Taryn because Callie was in love with the various cakes.

He patted his stomach. "I plan to have a slice of each."

"Maybe our groom's cakes will become sought after because of this wedding." That would be good for business. She drove to the bakery and parked in her spot in the alley. "Though most people will only have one."

"Callie isn't 'most people.'"

"No, she's not."

212

They exited the car.

The patio wasn't that crowded for a Friday night, but since the summer fair had been last weekend, that didn't surprise her. "Thanks for keeping me company."

"I'll see you inside."

"I'm not alone here."

"Humor me."

She could do that. They headed into the kitchen.

No one was there. Taryn preferred decorating cakes when no one was around. She'd planned to be gone only a few minutes, not have dinner. But she'd put away anything needing refrigeration.

Garrett tilted his head. "This isn't the music you usually play."

A romantic ballad played.

Taryn had left that running while she was gone. She washed her hands. "It isn't."

"Do you always listen to music while you work?" he asked.

"Yes." However, this special music was a part of her process. "But this is a playlist we use for weddings."

"Seriously?"

She nodded. "All the love songs and ballads set the tone and puts me in a wedding mode."

"I didn't know so much was involved."

"It might be me, but my grandpa did something similar when he decorated his cakes."

"A tradition passed down to you." Garrett leaned against the doorway. "Show me what you do next."

"This isn't entertainment."

"I find you entertaining."

She fought the urge to roll her eyes. "Your family is waiting for you."

"Except for Margot, they don't know I left," he countered. "Nervous?"

Taryn shrugged. "I'm not used to frosting on demand."

Wicked laughter lit his eyes. "Why Miss Lawson, that almost sounds dirty."

She held up a pastry bag. "Watch it, or you won't know what hit you. And it will be dirty. I mean messy."

"Go for it."

"Don't tempt me." She spun the cake to see where she'd left off. "Now, let me focus, or your sister will be disappointed."

WATCHING TARYN DECORATE mesmerized Garrett. He should have left when the bakery closed, but he had remained frozen as if his feet were glued to the floor. He couldn't get enough of her.

Her pinpoint-precision focus impressed him. As she piped a line of icing along the edge, her tongue stuck out of her mouth. She wasn't a pastry chef but an artist doing a live performance. Her medium was frosting, not paint. Instead of brushes, she used a spatula and bags with different-sized nozzles to create her magic.

A text notification sounded.

Garrett checked his phone. It was a text from a partner at

his firm.

> **JennJD:** *You're making rain again.*
>
> **Garrett:** *New client?*
>
> **JennJD:** *Yes! Can you talk right now?*
>
> **Garrett:** *Give me a minute. I'll call you.*

He put away his phone. Taryn was still hard at work.

"Is there a place I can make a call?" he asked. "It's for work."

"Sure." She motioned to a doorway. "Use my office. You can close the door."

"I don't need privacy."

She grinned. "I meant, so the music doesn't bother you."

He appreciated her thoughtfulness. "I won't be long."

Garrett sat at her desk and called Jenn, who picked up the phone on the first ring.

"When will you be home?" she asked in her no-nonsense voice, yet she could purr on command if that would sway the jury. The woman was a tiger in the courtroom.

"Sunday night. Why?"

"You reeled in a big fish even away on vacation."

That was one reason he'd been hired, and he kept making the big bucks. "Criminal or financial?"

"Billionaire arrested for bundling debt."

"Not illegal. Unless the Feds are changing the rules again, looking for another scapegoat."

"Bingo. Give yourself a gold star."

"He wants me?"

"You'll have a row of stars by the time we hang up."

"Fill me in."

Jenn did. When she finished, Garrett knew everything about Jedidiah Hoppes. "Tell my assistant when the meeting is, so it goes on my calendar."

"Have fun at the wedding tomorrow."

"Thanks. It should be a good time." Especially with Taryn there.

He disconnected from the call.

Garrett glanced around the office. Not as neat as her house, but he imagined she wasn't the only one who used it. His gaze landed on what appeared to be a vision board.

Hadn't she mentioned this to him?

Something about wanting to remodel and leave her mark on the bakery.

He peered closer—did a double take.

*Wow.*

This would do it.

Everything from the table and chairs to the painted wall coordinated with a new Lawson's Bakery logo and branding. Underneath the vision board were magazines with sticky tabs sticking out, catalogs, lists, budgets, furniture, and floor plans.

Sketches of signs that had a similar feel to the ones on the patio. Speaking of which, the branding of the new interior matched perfectly with the patio.

This would take time and money. Two things Taryn was short of right now, but the changes would help her compete against the other bakery.

Garrett flipped through a magazine and a catalog full of

page flags. She'd picked out the furniture, and it matched the photos on her vision board. Not surprising because that was how she operated, researching, leaving no stone unturned. He returned everything to its place.

He hoped she remodeled and left her mark the way she wanted. If anybody deserved success, Taryn did with her hard work, loyalty, and love of this bakery, its customers, and baking.

Back in the kitchen, she focused on the cakes and nothing else.

She stretched her arms overhead. "I need a break."

He would give her one. "Dance with me."

Her eyes widened. "Dance?"

"I don't understand your question."

"Do you want to dance with me?"

"Yes." Garrett knew what might sway her. "It's a way to warm up for the wedding. There's a dance floor, so we can safely assume there will be dancing."

"Does this line of reasoning sway juries?"

"Come on. What's stopping you?"

"I've never danced in a bakery. This would be a first for me."

"It's like dancing anywhere else." He held out his hand. "Take it."

As a popular John Legend song came on the radio, Garrett assumed the proper position and held her.

She touched his shoulder, but hesitation gleamed in her eyes.

"And we're off," he whispered.

They danced around the kitchen, careful not to bump into anything.

Holding her close felt so natural. Garrett never wanted to stop. His heart pounded. He tried to memorize everything about the moment—about her.

Taryn stared up at him. "What are you thinking?"

Dare he tell her the truth? "How much I'm enjoying this dance."

"Me, too. A good thing there will be more tomorrow."

Anticipation swelled. "I'm counting on it."

"I want to keep dancing, but I need to work on the cakes, or I'll be up all night."

"Can't have that."

Her face was so close to his. She moved forward, and he met her halfway. Garrett wasn't in any rush, even though he was leaving soon. He pulled her closer until she was up against him.

Right where she belonged.

Hands in her hair, his lips moved over hers.

*His.*

Not really, but he enjoyed pretending. And he would keep doing so as long as he could.

*Sunday*, a voice whispered.

The song ended, but Garrett didn't want to stop dancing.

Taryn let go of him. Her breathing was haggard, and her lips swollen.

"I'd love to keep…dancing, but the cakes await." Longing filled her eyes.

He kissed her cheek. "I'll see if there's anything I need to pick up before I walk home."

She smiled up at him. "Thanks for the company and the dance. I can't wait until tomorrow."

"Me, either." He raised her hand to his mouth and kissed each knuckle. "As soon as you finish the cakes, go to bed. You're going to need all your energy for tomorrow night. We're going to dance the night away."

# Chapter Eighteen

SATURDAY MORNING, JAYDEN helped Taryn load the cakes into her car. He would follow her over, help her unload, and then go to the bakery to work with Carl. She would run home, change clothes, and return in time for the ceremony.

"It's a beautiful day for a wedding." Jayden carried one of the groom's cakes. "I hate we won't be open tonight, but everyone's burnt out from working double and split shifts."

"We'll take a hit, but everyone needs a break." Herself included, and she hadn't wanted to miss the wedding.

Jayden gently closed her hatchback. "See you over there."

A few minutes later, she parked at the winery on the outskirts of town. She hopped out of the car and went to check out the layout.

Two steps inside, she froze.

The room was empty. None of the banquet tables were set up. No cake table. Nothing.

A man ran into the room. "You're the baker."

"Yes."

"I'm Tomas, the manager." He pulled out a table. "There's been a...misunderstanding."

"With staffing?"

He blew out a breath. "Someone called last night claiming to be the groom and canceled the wedding. No one notified me, but they took it upon themselves to call everyone scheduled to work today and tell them not to come in. I phoned Mr. Winslow this morning to see if he'd called, but he said he hadn't."

Nick Baxter. Taryn grimaced. It had to be him. The guy had it out for Brandt and anyone involved in his wedding, including her.

"I notified the employees, but some had made other plans, so we reached out to the catering company. We're a little behind, but as soon as people show up, we'll have everything ready."

Maybe, but she could call others now.

"Give me a minute." Tomas's breathing was ragged and his face red. "I need to bring out the linens. Those are ready, but aren't out here."

As he hurried into a room, she sent a text to Garrett and a few others, telling them what happened. Anna was the maid of honor, so Taryn didn't notify her. She didn't want Callie to worry.

Taryn tucked her phone in her pocket. "What can I do to help?"

Tomas's eyes gleamed. He pulled out a floor plan for the room. "Set up the cake table?"

She took a picture of the paper. "Of course. I asked a few friends to come over and help until your staff arrives."

He wiped his eyes. "Thank you. This has never happened. The wedding coordinator was on her way to Seattle. She's turned around, but…"

"It'll work out." Taryn sounded more confident than she felt, but she would not let Nick Baxter ruin her friends' wedding.

"What the…" Jayden stared in disbelief.

"Nick struck again." She showed him her phone. "We need to make this room look like that, starting with the cake table."

Jayden rubbed his forehead. "Whatever you say, Boss. But we can't leave the cakes in the car."

"I forgot." Which wasn't like her. "Let's put them on the piano for now."

They carried in the cakes and set up the table. Both Taryn and Jayden had experience with table skirting, or they would have been in trouble.

He straightened the bottom. "Is this where it should be?"

She checked the layout. "Yes."

"I'll help you with the wedding cake and then work with Tomas on the tables."

"Sounds like a plan."

Together they placed the wedding cake in the center of the table. Taryn still had some decorations to add to it. "Go help Tomas."

She removed a pastry bag from her box of supplies.

Two hands touched her shoulders.

Taryn jumped.

"It's me." Garrett kissed the top of her head. "Thanks for sounding the alarm. I brought my brothers, dad, and

Brandt's dad. None of the moms or Margot know what's going on."

"Good."

He glanced at his family, who rolled round tables into place. "Don't worry. We'll have this set up, and no one will be the wiser."

"How do you know I'm worried?" she asked.

He touched the spot between her eyebrows. "You get these two lines."

Garrett was as bad as Jayden. "I'm not as worried now that you're here."

"Any idea how this happened?"

"A man called last night claiming to be the groom and canceled the wedding. Sounds like something Nick would do."

Garrett's nostrils flared. "After we're finished setting up, I'll see if there's a phone number we can follow up on."

"You can do that?"

"My firm has investigators on staff. They are some of the best in the business. If they can't figure out who did this, a strongly worded letter with way too much legalese from Brandt's attorney will be sent to Mr. Baxter."

"Is his attorney standing in this room?"

Garrett grinned. "Maybe."

Affection overflowed for this man. "Thank you. Now, I need to work on the cake."

"Have fun." He kissed her cheek.

The setup continued. As soon as Taryn had the cakes in place, she sent Jayden to the bakery, so Carl wasn't alone, and she helped the others. More winery staff and catering people arrived, including a harried wedding coordinator named Chelsea, who shrieked when she saw what hadn't been done.

Two hours later, Pippa arrived at her scheduled time, and soon the centerpieces and other flowers were in place.

Callie's dad called everyone together. "I want to thank Taryn for letting us know what was happening and thank each of you for helping us make sure Callie and Brandt get the wedding they deserve. Drinks are on me tonight."

People cheered.

"The entire wedding is on you, Dad," Flynn said.

Everyone laughed.

"Now, go get ready." Mr. Andrews glanced at his watch. "The wedding starts in less than an hour."

Garrett grabbed her hand. "We don't have a lot of time, but I want you to save me a dance."

"Just one?"

He kissed her forehead. "All of them."

Her stomach fluttered. "My dance card belongs to you."

"I'm going to hold you to that."

Her grin spread to the tips of her toes. "You'd better."

AS GARRETT SAT in the first row of chairs on the bride's side of the aisle, in between his two brothers, the sun beat down. The temperature was in the eighties, and sweat dripped down his back. He didn't mind. His tuxedo could be dry-cleaned. Luckily, the roof of the gazebo provided shade for three of the most important people there. Six, if he counted the wedding party—Anna, Sam, and Rex.

The officiant, a boisterous man who didn't need a microphone, wiped his forehead with a pink handkerchief that matched his tie. With his bushy white beard, he would fit on a Hallmark Christmas card, wearing a red suit and sitting on a sleigh pulled by reindeer, but his gray suit would make for better wedding photos.

Callie's eyes gleamed. She hadn't stopped smiling since she walked down the aisle. Her stunning white gown made her look like a princess, especially with the diamond tiara holding her veil in place. Brandt wiped his face more than once. The guy glowed as much as his bride and couldn't stop staring at Callie. Anna wore a pale pink one-shouldered gown. The color matched the roses in Callie's bridal bouquet and the floral swags on the gazebo. Sam, the best man, rocked a black tux. Rex, however, outshone them all but the bride. He looked as handsome as Callie claimed he would in his bow tie with a satin ring pillow attached. He sat patiently next to the groom as if being in a wedding happened every day. No leash required.

Garrett imagined himself getting married in that gazebo, standing with his bride. Not a nameless, faceless woman, either.

Heart pounding, he glanced over his shoulder to where Taryn sat with Raine from the coffee shop. The two women dabbed their eyes with tissues.

When Callie said her wedding vows, Garrett's eyes stung. He blinked before rubbing them. He wanted to blame the wetness on pollen, but it was all his sister.

Keaton elbowed him. "Mom has a tissue."

"Shhhh," Flynn said.

Garrett focused on their sister. He couldn't believe she was getting married. He remembered her following him around the house with a stuffed cat in one hand and a robotic dog in the other. That didn't seem so long ago, even if it had been over two decades.

"I now pronounce you husband and wife." The officiant grinned widely. "You may kiss the bride."

Callie and Brandt kissed.

Guests applauded and cheered, but none louder than Garrett, Flynn, and Keaton.

"Nice wedding," Flynn said. "But if Brandt hurts her, he'll wish he were never born."

"Times that by three," Keaton added.

Garrett covered his ears with his hands. "La, la, la, la, la. I can't hear anything you're saying."

All three of them laughed.

As they held hands, the newlyweds made their way up the aisle as "All You Need Is Love" played. The song was familiar from one of Callie's favorite movies, *Love Actually*. The two beamed brightly. Even Rex smiled.

"The youngest got married first." Keaton shook his head. "I didn't see that happening."

Flynn shrugged. "When do the three of us have time to date, let alone get serious?"

Garrett nodded. "Truth."

Though he'd dated Taryn, he'd also been on vacation, so

his brother might have a point.

"Odds suggest the oldest will be next." Keaton came up with weird calculations and facts. Not that he taught math, but it must be a professor thing.

Flynn held up his hands. "Not me."

Garrett's money was on Keaton. Well, Margot. But he wouldn't admit that to his younger brother. "Time will tell."

Flynn's gaze followed the newlyweds. "I hope Callie and Brandt have kids sooner rather than later to take the pressures off us. As long as Mom and Dad keep working, it shouldn't be a problem, but as soon as they retire…"

Garrett and Keaton both nodded.

"Boys," his mother called, motioning them over. "Time for photos."

As Garrett followed his brothers, he searched for Taryn but didn't see her. No worries, he would find her at the reception and claim his dance.

All of them.

As Callie and Brandt danced, Garrett sipped champagne. He sat at the family table while Taryn was at another with friends from the First Avenue Business Association.

Margot sat in the empty chair next to him. "You should invite Taryn to sit with you."

"Callie assigned the seating."

"That was before you and Taryn—"

He straightened. "Before we what?"

"Worked together on the booth."

The woman wouldn't give up. "Good catch."

Margot's eyes twinkled. "It was, wasn't it?"

Garrett laughed.

"I hope you plan to dance with Taryn. Without her help earlier, Callie and Brandt would have been disappointed."

He turned toward Margot. "How did you find out?"

"Oh, sweet barrister, I know everything that happens in Silver Falls. I'm like that part in the center of a bicycle wheel where all the spokes meet. That's how I get all my info."

"You're not only the town matchmaker but also the head gossiper."

She gave him a cheeky grin. "Someone has to do it."

Garrett raised his glass to her. "Welcome to the family."

"Same to you. We added two doctors, two lawyers, a professor, and a dog whisperer with one 'I do.' Given Brandt's the only kid in the family, the boy did well."

"So did Callie."

"For sure." Margot's mouth formed a perfect o. "I'm not sure if your people called you, but the sheriff had enough evidence to visit Nick Baxter this evening."

"I turned off my phone." Garrett pulled his out of his pocket and turned it on. Notifications popped on his screen. He scanned them. Nick had gotten sloppy this time, and his investigator's information had been provided to the police. "Your sources are correct."

"Let's hope it finally stops him. He's had it out for Brandt ever since my nephew wouldn't get involved in some business deal in December. I'm sorry Taryn got dragged into it by making their wedding cake."

"Everything worked out."

"And it'll work out even better if you ask her to dance."

"No matchmaking."

"I said dance, not kiss her until you can't breathe or see straight."

Garrett wouldn't mind doing that later. He stood. "I want to get the first dance out of the way."

So he couldn't wait for all the other ones.

As he approached the table where Taryn sat, Raine nudged her.

Taryn looked his way, and her smile lit up her face.

His heart crashed into his rib cage as if he'd slammed on the brake pedal to stop from rear-ending someone on the 405. Garrett's mouth went dry. She captivated him.

Taryn stood and extended her arm. "You owe me a dance."

He laced his fingers with hers, leading her toward the dance floor, where a DJ played music.

As if on cue, the song changed.

She inhaled sharply.

No worries, it was another slow dance, which is what he wanted—any excuse to hold Taryn in his arms.

"Listen." She tilted her head. "They're playing our song."

Wait. What? The music sounded familiar, but... "We have a song?"

Taryn nodded. "This will be the second time we've danced to 'All of Me' by John Legend in twenty-four hours. I believe that counts as a song."

"Good point." Garrett took her in his arms and moved

with the music the way they had last night. "I've never had a song with someone before."

"Me, either."

Garrett brushed his lips over her hair. He could get used to this.

Who was he kidding? Garrett wanted to get used to this.

He enjoyed dancing with her, but the dance floor was crowded. Garrett preferred being at the bakery where it was more romantic with just the two of them.

He twirled her around, and that was when it hit him.

Garrett wasn't ready to say goodbye. He'd felt twinges of this in December, but he'd brushed them aside. He didn't want to do the same this time. He wanted...more.

Things had gotten serious fast. It should scare him, but he was okay with that.

With her.

She sighed. "This is nice."

"It is." But how would a long-distance relationship work? His job was all-consuming when a case went to trial. She gave her all to the bakery.

Saying goodbye would be the smartest thing for their careers, but Taryn brought something into his life he hadn't known was missing. Something he hadn't known he needed. Seeing Callie get married, declaring her love and fidelity to Brandt, struck a chord inside Garrett. He wanted that with Taryn, and if he let her go again, said goodbye when he left on Sunday, it would never happen.

Besides, who knew what her dad intended to do?

Now might be the perfect time for Taryn to try something new, someplace new.

Like L.A.

With him.

She had the skills and would be in high demand. They could make this work.

All he had to do was ask her to come with him.

# Chapter Nineteen

WEDDING GUESTS FORMED two lines, standing shoulder to shoulder, ten feet apart. Taryn stood next to Garrett, his arm touching hers. From the ceremony to the end of the reception, today had been magical, not only for Callie and Brandt but everyone attending their wedding.

In the line across from them, Margot wiggled her shoulders. "This is so fun."

And it was.

Not only fun but also romantic.

The event—well, minus the rush earlier to set up the reception—made Taryn wistful for more nights like this. Her feet ached from all the dancing, but she didn't mind at all. A part of her wished tonight would never end.

Anna and Raine passed out three-feet-long sparklers to each person. Flynn and Keaton followed with lighters.

"How did you get out of helping with the farewell?" Taryn whispered in Garrett's ear.

"I told them I needed to be with my unofficial plus-one."

She loved how his warm breath caressed her skin, giving her the best possible kind of chills. "Unofficial plus-one? Never heard of that term before."

He kissed her neck. "I made it up."

Tingles shot through her. "Be careful, or we might burn ourselves with the sparklers."

His gaze, reflecting the bright sparks, met hers. "I'll take my chances."

Garrett brushed his lips across hers.

"Hold the sparklers in the air," the photographer who stood at the far end shouted, breaking the spell.

Everyone raised theirs, and the result was a stunning tunnel of sparks for the bride and groom to exit the reception.

Smiling big, Callie and Brandt held hands and made their way through the tunnel as the photographer took photos. People cheered them on.

"Congrats."

"Best wishes."

"Bon voyage."

"Don't do anything I wouldn't do."

"Congratulations."

Callie and Brandt stopped near the end of the tunnel and kissed.

A roar went up from the crowd.

So sweet. Taryn sighed.

Garrett sighed. "They're perfect together."

Something inside Taryn's heart shifted. She wanted that. Not perfection. That didn't exist. Nor did she want a huge wedding that must have cost Mr. and Mrs. Andrews a small fortune. No, Taryn wanted to find the forever kind of love Callie had found with her new husband.

Unless…

Taryn glanced at Garrett, who focused on the couple. Maybe she would find it with him. Given everything he helped her through, they were off to a good start. And what she felt for him was more than friendship. He'd wanted to make amends, but he hadn't stopped when he'd done that. He'd stepped up, continuing to help her. His concern over her business, the fair, and Brecken showed what kind of man Garrett Andrews was.

Not perfect, but kindhearted.

A man who loved his family.

Could he love her someday?

Taryn shook her head.

That was a silly question with him in California and her in Washington, especially when she'd known from the start he wasn't here to stay. He was leaving tomorrow night.

What else could she do but say goodbye?

Again.

She half laughed, not a joyful sound, but a bittersweet one.

Despite her issues with her parents and the bakery, her life was in Silver Falls. Could she start over elsewhere? Yes, but California—especially Los Angeles—was larger than Portland, where she'd gone to culinary school and done her internship. If she hadn't enjoyed living there, how would she like somewhere more urban?

As the newlyweds laughed at something the photographer said, they glanced over their shoulders and waved.

Callie blew a kiss. "Thanks, everyone."

Brandt helped her into an idling limousine before facing the crowd. "Thanks for making this the best wedding ever."

He climbed into the back seat. The driver closed the door, and less than a minute later, the vehicle pulled away from the curb.

Taryn, Garrett, his family, and guests waved until the limousine's taillights disappeared.

"I can't believe they're taking a six-week-long honeymoon," Mrs. Jones said to her husband, who waved his sparkler as if he were seven, not seventy. "I had no idea that was possible."

"If I sell the hardware store, we'll go on a long second honeymoon."

The older woman kissed his wrinkled cheek. "When not if."

The man laughed. "Now, you'll hold me to it."

Mrs. Jones shook her head. "You're not getting any younger."

As the two kissed, a longing grew inside Taryn.

*I want that.*

But did Garrett?

*Too soon.*

It was way too soon.

Logically, she knew that. They'd spent four weeks in the same town, and not all that time had been at once. But tell those facts to her heart, which was in a mood for another wedding. One where she wore the gown, carried the bouquet, and had a wedding band slid on her ring finger.

She gulped.

"Do you have to do any of the cleanup?" Garrett asked.

"No." And she was thankful for that. "Once we set up the cake, we're done. The caterer took care of slicing and serving the pieces. That's why I could enjoy the reception."

*With you.*

"Come with me." He entwined his fingers with hers and led her to the courtyard where a three-tiered fountain spewed water thirty feet in the air while multicolored lights flashed on and off in a choreographed dance. It had proved a perfect photo op for the newlyweds and guests. The spot was as lovely now.

He raised her hand to his mouth and kissed the top of it. "Tonight was fun."

"It was." The best part was being with him. Garrett looked like a model in his tuxedo, but his appearance was only a tiny part of his appeal. Not just anyone would work nonstop in ninety-degree heat to help her redo the booth at the eleventh hour. "Your sister is a beautiful bride."

"The cake was delicious."

"Which one?"

His grin spread. "All of them. Obviously the guests agreed because not much is left."

"I hope the bride and groom enjoyed them." That was what made an event successful. Sure, Taryn wanted all the guests to enjoy them, but she wanted the bride and groom, Callie and Brandt, to be happy with their choice of hiring Lawson's Bakery.

"Callie and Brandt loved them." Garrett tucked strands of Taryn's hair behind her ear. "You're an incredible baker."

"I am, aren't I?" she teased before curtseying. "Thanks."

"I've enjoyed these two weeks with you."

*Uh-oh.* That sounded like goodbye. Her pulse kicked up.

"Me, too." She wasn't sure what was coming, but she wanted to prepare herself mentally. "Even more so than December."

"This has been different." He stared into her eyes. "I go home tomorrow."

"I know." This must be goodbye. She kept a smile on her face, even though she'd wanted to spend more time with him. But his family was still here, and Callie and Brandt were having brunch with their immediate families tomorrow. Garrett needed to be with them. "I can't thank you enough for all you did for me."

"I enjoyed myself."

"Same."

"Which is why I won't ghost you again."

Hope blossomed inside her. Maybe this wasn't goodbye after all. "I'm so happy to hear that because I don't want to be ghosted again."

"I've been thinking about us."

She wiggled her toes. "I like the sound of us."

"Me, too."

The lights from the fountain made her think of them standing under the northern lights. If only they could do that someday.

"That's why I want you to come to L.A.," he said.

Yes. She forced herself not to bounce on her tiptoes. "I'll plan a visit."

"No."

Taryn flinched. "You don't want me to visit?"

"I want you in L.A." He tugged at his bow tie. "I'm doing this all wrong. What I mean is, I want you to move to L.A."

Her brain tried to comprehend what he was saying. Tried and failed. "Move to L.A.?"

Excitement flashed on his face. "It's a perfect solution. With your skills, you could find a job at any bakery or restaurant. Even a hotel."

"I have a job."

"In Silver Falls, but I'm in L.A. I want you with me."

Wow. This wasn't what Taryn expected to hear. Not that she expected him to give up everything for her and move to Washington state. Maybe she thought they'd decide to date long-distance and go from there, but he wasn't declaring his love or offering any sort of commitment other than wanting her there.

A part of her wanted to throw her arms around Garrett and never let go. The other part wanted to back away and put as much distance as she could between them. He was deciding her future without asking for her input. The same way her parents were doing with the bakery. "I want to be with you, but..."

His intense gaze locked on hers. "What?"

"The bakery is my family legacy."

"You don't know what your dad has planned."

"I didn't, but we spoke on Monday. He and my mom plan to sell the bakery. They think I shouldn't run it so I can get married and have kids."

"Old-fashioned."

"Yes, that...surprised me."

"So if he won't turn over the bakery—"

"I asked him to sell the bakery to me. He hasn't given me an answer, but I applied for a small business loan."

"You want to stay in Silver Falls?"

She hated seeing the disappointment in his eyes. "It's home."

"L.A. is my home."

"Yes, but you're asking me to give up everything. The same as my parents."

"It's not the same. I care about you."

Care, not love. It didn't surprise her because they hadn't known each other that long. "My mom and dad do, too, even if they have a funny way of showing it."

His lips thinned. "Where does that leave us?"

Good question. Taryn wished she had an answer. "Aren't you licensed to practice in other states besides California?"

"Yes, but I'm a partner in the firm. I need to be in L.A."

"And I need to be here in Silver Falls. If my parents don't sell Lawson's to me, then I'll start my own bakery. That's the dream, and I want to pursue it."

"Does it matter where you open your bakery? Does it have to be here?"

"I don't know." But she wouldn't rush the choice. Not when there were so many uncertainties with her parents. She took a step away from him. "Whether or not the Lawson's Bakery is ever mine, I need to be here and see this through."

"Don't you want to see where this goes between us?"

"More than anything, but at what cost?"

"What do you suggest?"

Relief flowed through her. At least Garrett was asking her opinion about this. A good thing she had one. "What if we see how things go with you in L.A. and me here?"

"You heard how Raine talked about long-distance relationships."

"I did." But Taryn was the one being asked to give up everything. That was too much at this point. She stared at the cement.

"What are you thinking?" he asked.

That they'd shared their hopes, dreams, failures. Hadn't he listened to hers? Or maybe he didn't care.

No, she didn't want to believe that was it. "Look, I get that Lawson's Bakery isn't like the fancy ones in L.A. or as successful as your firm. But it's been in my family for three generations. I can't pack up and leave without fighting for what's mine."

"Neither can I. I'm a rainmaker. Clients hire the firm because of me. Our employees rely on us to keep bringing in business."

"So does everyone who works at the bakery. I don't have a company worth of employees, but Jayden, Carl, Finley, Brecken, and Mandy matter."

"My reputation is tied with the firm."

"I understand that, and I'm not asking you to move to Silver Falls. But I want you to understand the bakery means everything to me and why I need to be here."

"I know that, but I can imagine something long-term with you. The possibility of a future together."

"Same. So what if we give the long-distance thing a try?"

"Being in the same city would be easier."

"Yes, but we've spent what? Four weeks together total, separated by nearly six months. It's too soon for one of us to uproot our lives."

He said nothing.

"Garrett?" she asked.

"You're right." He didn't sound that certain. "But I'm not sure how it'll work."

"Neither am I, but if this really means something to us, we'll make it work somehow."

At least, she hoped so.

SUNDAY MORNING, GARRETT checked the availability of flights. He wanted to move his flight from tonight to tomorrow or Tuesday, but everything was full.

A knock sounded, and the door opened. Flynn walked in.

Garrett glared at his brother. "I didn't tell you it was okay to come in."

Flynn raised an eyebrow as if someone would dare complain about him. Typical of his big brother, who acted as if the world revolved around him. It did at the hospital where he performed surgery and was treated like a rock star by residents and staff. "If we were at home, I wouldn't knock."

"But we're not."

He rolled his eyes before tilting his head. His trademark move annoyed Garrett and Keaton, but Callie thought Flynn had the bored, entitled pretty-boy look down, so if being a surgeon didn't work out, he would make a fortune as a lifestyle influencer.

"You were supposed to be downstairs ten minutes ago." Flynn sounded put out and exhausted, as if he'd climbed Mount Rainier instead of a flight of stairs. The same as he did when he'd been young.

Even though they were in their thirties—except for Callie—some things never changed. "Why is it when we all get together, it's like we're kids again?"

"Because no matter how old we get, Mom and Dad still see us as teens, tweens, kids, and toddlers who never do as they're told."

Sounded about right. "What's going on downstairs?"

"Mom has a surprise for us. She said it would be fun."

Their mom was loving and kind, but being a brainy doctor was at the core of her identity. Growing up, "fun" meant something educational unless it were a game she would be assured of winning. Most assumed they inherited their competitive streak from their dad, but he wasn't nearly as bad as their mom. "Tell me she doesn't want us to play a game of Operation."

Flynn laughed. "I don't think so, but I might beat her now."

Garrett stood. He would pack later.

Downstairs, he learned Margot had planned the activity. She was making Callie and Brandt a quilt. Mr. and Mrs. Winslow had made their parts when they'd been in town for the Fourth of July. Now it was the Andrews' turn. And it went over as well as it would have if they'd been kids.

Flynn played the dutiful, oldest son. Garrett did his best while trying to keep from laughing the entire time. And Keaton complained and somehow injured his index finger.

Their mom took pictures. "We're making memories."

"She needs grandkids," Keaton muttered.

"I heard that." But Mom didn't appear deterred. "It looks like Callie has a head start on giving us grands. Unless Garrett has something to tell us about how cozy he's gotten with a certain baker in town."

*Ugh.* Just kill him now. He pressed too hard on the sewing machine's pedal and lifted his foot. "Let's focus on quilting so I don't make a mistake."

"She's a smart one," his dad chimed in. "Bakes like a dream. And is pretty, too."

Taryn was all those things. "We're giving long-distance dating a try. Her life is in Silver Falls, and mine is in L.A."

"You two made a cute couple," his mom said. "But that might be rough with your job."

Garrett agreed. He still didn't know if this would work. That bothered him more than he wanted to admit, because he couldn't see how this would work out. "Emphasis on try."

Which meant another goodbye might be in their future.

No, he didn't want to think about that. "We're taking on a new client. It could be huge for the firm with lots of publicity. So we'll see what happens with Taryn."

"I hope it works out," his dad said.

Garrett, too, because he had no idea what he would do if it didn't.

# Chapter Twenty

TARYN THREW HERSELF into work at the bakery, not taking days off and working more than one shift most days. She straightened the counter by the cash register. Who cared if she'd done it earlier this morning? And would likely do it again before the evening rush? But the busier she kept herself, the less she missed Garrett.

Okay, not really, but she kept hoping it worked.

He'd only been gone for a week, but each day dragged. He was busy himself, so they barely had time to talk except to say goodnight. Twice had been via text. But this was still new. They would get the hang of it soon.

The door pinged.

Anna entered, carrying two cups from Raine's place.

Taryn grinned. "Are you taking a break from making pups look beautiful?"

"You know it." Anna handed a cup to her. "Here you go."

"Thanks, but what's this for?"

"Raine sent it over. She knows how difficult long-distance relationships are."

No kidding, and Taryn's was at the beginning. "That

was sweet of her."

Anna raised her cup. "To more time with your hottie lawyer."

"Cheers." Taryn sipped. That hit the spot. She lowered her cup. "Mocha is a favorite."

"Raine must have everyone's favorite drink order memorized. She wanted to come over, but she's too busy." Anna motioned to the display case. Most trays were less than half full. "Looks like you are, too."

"Business has quadrupled since the summer fair." That had been over a week ago.

"Did you hear that Nick and Robin's house went on the market?"

"Yes. He's worn out his welcome around here and in Summit Ridge. I'm not sure how Brandt stood to be in the same room as Nick. I couldn't. But at least the other bakery is playing fair now."

"The recipe and idea funnel is permanently closed."

"Yes. They raised their prices. Couple that with the hits on their reputation, and people aren't driving there as much."

"It must make you happy having customers return."

"I'm carefully optimistic." The bakery had suffered from months of lower sales, but Taryn knew they would recover. But she'd learned a valuable lesson. "Those who left us purchase based on prices, not loyalty, so I'll keep that in mind and add in an occasional sale. I have some ideas to discuss with my dad."

Taryn was meeting with her parents tonight. They still

hadn't mentioned her buying the bakery. Still, she wanted to review some pricing strategies she'd researched and suggest her dad promote Jayden. He should be a manager. The bakery needed two—her and Jayden. The raise and title were well earned and thanks for him sticking with them, but Margot had heard Rachelle might be pregnant. No official announcement had been made, so Taryn wasn't saying a word. But she knew how long they'd been trying and was thrilled for them.

Anna took another sip. "You've got a brain for business."

"I'm learning all I can." Taryn put on a new glove and removed a blueberry scone—one of Anna's favorites—stuck it in a bag, and handed it to her friend. She would drop off something for Raine later. "Here you go."

"Thank you." Anna peeked inside. "I should bring over coffee more often."

"I'll be here." Taryn only wished Garrett was there, too. But it wasn't fair of her to ask, just as it hadn't been fair of him. She had to believe they would find a way.

"Well, I should get back to the shop. Callie left me in charge during her honeymoon."

"I hope they are having a wonderful time."

"I prefer to stand beside a grooming table than behind the front counter. But it's the least I can do. Callie deserves the long break. And it'll be good for her and Brandt."

"We should grab dinner. See if Raine wants to join us. Pippa, too."

"I'd love that. I'll find out when people are free." Anna grabbed a napkin from the dispenser. "Talk to you soon."

The door beeped when she opened it and again when it closed.

Taryn drank her mocha. This hit the spot. It also reminded her she should make more time for her friends. All relationships needed attention, not be taken for granted and only nurtured when convenient.

She half laughed. Isn't that what she'd initially and mistakenly thought she was to Garrett—a convenience?

Taryn picked up a rag from the bleach bucket under the counter and walked to the eating area, where she washed tables before returning and removing her gloves.

Jayden headed out of the kitchen. "If you need more to clean, please come over to my house."

"Be careful, or you might find me at your doorstep with a dust rag and vacuum cleaner."

"Don't say that in front of Rachelle, or she'll be expecting you."

That would have been the perfect opening for a baby announcement, but Jayden said nothing. His facial expression remained neutral, too. Margot's gossip could be wrong this time.

He leaned against the counter. "Have you talked to Garrett?"

Her throat tightened, and the ache in her chest grew. "Yesterday. We plan to talk later."

"Good."

She hated to ask, but curiosity got the best of her. "Do you think it'll last?"

"Only you can answer that. How much do you want it to

last?"

"Badly."

"Then don't give up. Rachelle and I were apart for two years while I finished college, and she went through the fire academy. Let nothing—that includes distance—get in the way."

"Good advice."

He laughed. "It's easier to give than follow."

"I'm going to pretend you didn't say that."

"Or you could move to Los Angeles."

"You followed Rachelle for her job."

"Yes, but we've never had a traditional marriage."

"That's not a bad thing." Especially considering how her parents viewed matrimony.

"It works for us. You and Garrett have to figure what works for you guys. It might take time."

She needed to hear this. "I keep wishing it would be a quick fix."

"If only." Jayden put on gloves and pulled out a large pink bakery box. He filled it with pastries. Someone must have phoned in an order. "Giving up is easy. Perseverance is key."

"I'll remember that."

Jayden studied her as if he couldn't decide if he were making fudge and trying to determine if she'd reached the soft-ball stage without a candy thermometer. "There's nothing wrong with wanting what seems impossible."

She wanted two things that seemed that way—Garrett and the bakery.

"You also might learn about yourself through this."

"How to make a long-distance relationship work?"

"That, and what do you need in your life to be happy."

"Thanks." She smiled at her friend and coworker. "Rachelle is lucky to have you."

He laughed. "I only know this stuff from messing up with her."

Would Garrett ever say that about her someday?

Taryn sighed.

Jayden handed her a snickerdoodle cookie. "It looks like you need this."

"Thanks."

"Keep believing in the two of you. That's all you can do."

"Besides, eat cookies."

He laughed. "That, too."

"I can do both." She bit into the cookie. Now, if she could do the first as well as she did the second.

"DELICIOUS DINNER, MOM." That night, Taryn sat in her parents' kitchen and sipped from her iced tea. She listened to stories about their cruise. Not once had the bakery been mentioned. Were they saving the best for last? She nearly choked. But it would be better to let them bring it up. She swallowed. "I'm happy you had such a great vacation."

Her father wiped his mouth. "You should take one."

"I'm planning a trip to Los Angeles, but I have to figure out the logistics." Taryn wanted to make sure Garrett wasn't in the middle of a trial or that intense prep period he'd mentioned.

Her parents glanced at each other.

Her dad cleared his throat. "I'm happy to fill in if you're low on staff."

"Thanks, Dad. I'd appreciate that. Though I hired Brecken's sister, Mandy."

He nodded. "Sweet kid. Loved ginger snaps when she was little."

"Still does." Taryn laughed. "We need two or three more people, especially with Finley's and Brecken's availability changing in the fall. You should also promote Jayden to be a manager. He's earned it. I wanted to do that months ago until the Summit Ridge Bakery got in the way."

Her father shifted in his chair. "About that."

Taryn held her breath.

"I told them no," he said.

She seemed to sink. The relief was palpable.

"Your mother made me see I may have been wrong to decide what your future should be."

Taryn mouthed a thank you to her mom across the table.

"I still think running a business will be too much when you have a family, but I can't wait for you to prove me wrong."

Taryn gripped the chair seat. "Does that mean..."

"Lawson's is yours if you want it."

"I do." The words burst from her lips, and then she remembered Garrett. "I—"

"What, sweetheart?" Her mom leaned forward.

Taryn bit her lip. "Could I please make a phone call?"

Her parents exchanged a glance.

"Sure," her father said.

"Thanks, Dad." She stood. "I'll make it quick."

Out on the front porch, she called Garrett. "Pick up. Please pick up."

"Taryn?" Garrett asked. "Are you okay?"

Was she? Her pulse raced. She struggled to catch her breath. "No. Yes. My dad said Lawson's is mine if I want it."

"Your dream come true."

"Part of the dream." She gripped the phone. "You're the other half, and...I...I love you."

The air rushed out of her lungs.

Silence, uncomfortable and gnawing, filled the line.

Oh, no. "It's too soon. I'm sorry. I shouldn't have—"

"Breathe, Taryn."

She did. That helped her regain control.

"Better?" he asked.

"Yes, thanks." Except she didn't know what to say next. "I miss you, and if I take over the bakery fully..."

"You're considering that?" He sounded shocked.

She was, too. "I-I don't know what to do. I feel as if I say yes to one then I'm saying no to another. I wish there were a way to say yes to both. What would you do?"

"Other than tell you to pack a suitcase and catch the next flight to LAX?"

The humor in his voice suggested he was joking. "Yes, other than that."

"Owning Lawson's Bakery is your dream. Say yes to

that."

Her heart sank. "Is that what you want?"

"It's what you need. That's the most important thing."

Her heart roared in her ears. "What about us? Will there still be an us?"

The silence made her tremble. "I want there to be."

"Me, too. So nothing has changed."

Other than her saying *I love you* and not getting any response, positive or negative. "I'd like to visit. If you text me some dates that are good for you, I'll book a flight."

"You want to make this work."

She couldn't tell if he was happy or shocked. "I really want this to work, which is why I wanted to talk to you before giving my parents an answer about the bakery."

A beat passed. And another.

"Say yes. I appreciate you telling me. But promise me, you'll tell your parents yes."

That was what Taryn hoped he would say. Except now, she didn't know how to feel about it. "O-kay."

She didn't trust herself to say more.

"I'm still at work," he said. "It's going to be a late night. But we'll talk more this weekend."

"Good night." Taryn had to force the word from her tight throat. She disconnected from the call.

*I love you.*

She prayed that wasn't the first and last time she said those words.

But she couldn't stay out here all night. Her parents were waiting for her, and she needed to tell them yes.

Yes.

She blew out a breath.

Yes to her dream of owning the bakery.

That was what Garrett wanted her to do. It was what she wanted too. But she also wanted more.

Taryn opened the door and entered her parents' house.

# Chapter Twenty-One

G ARRETT SAT IN his office. The sky was a beautiful blend of blue, purple, and orange. Others had gone home, but this place was still buzzing with activity. He enjoyed the atmosphere—the noise. His condo was too quiet. Not that it mattered. Whether he was there or at work, Taryn was never far from his mind. He missed her.

Callie and Brandt.

Rex.

Margot.

Angus and Sadie.

The bakery.

Silver Falls.

But he missed Taryn most of all.

The selfies from Callie and Brandt with heart eyes and beaming smiles only made Garrett miss Taryn more. Oh, he was thrilled for his sister. She was living her best life with a great guy who loved her as much as she loved him. Whereas Garrett, who everyone claimed was so successful, was barely going through the motions because of a small-town baker.

*I love you.*

Even though he'd hung up from her call nearly half an

hour ago, Taryn's words echoed through his brain. He'd been stunned. He hadn't known how to reply. The obvious answer was to tell her he loved her, except that would feel too quid pro quo.

His assistant poked her head into his office. "Mr. Hoppes is here for his meeting."

Time to pull himself together. Garrett adjusted his tie. "Thanks. And you're here late again. Go home."

"Thanks."

A few minutes later, Garrett entered the conference room, surprised to see only one man seated at the table. He thought more people would be there.

Jedidiah Hoppes, fifty-four with more gray than brown strands of hair, stood. The billionaire wore an expertly tailored suit, subdued silk tie, and crisp dress shirt. He'd founded an investment firm and was currently out on bail and not considered a flight risk.

"Jedidiah Hoppes, but everyone calls me Jed." He extended his arm. "It's nice to meet you finally. I hope you enjoyed your sister's wedding."

"Garrett Andrews." Garrett shook hands. Jed's grip was strong. "I did. The team updated me on your case. I'm sorry I postponed our meeting last week."

"That's okay. Something with my family came up anyway." Jed sat and glanced around the room with its expensive furniture and artwork. "I was told this was the hotshot firm and the best in L.A."

"It is."

Jed chuckled. "Everyone has been wonderful, especially

Jenn."

Jenn, a managing partner, had a genius-level I.Q. and was charismatic enough to have jurists eating out her hand with a smile.

"Happy to hear that." Garrett took a seat across from him.

Jed steepled his fingers. "I spoke to several firms before signing with yours, but this one came out on top. I'm impressed with the representation I've received so far. But I wanted to meet you one-on-one."

"That's smart. Not everyone clicks." Garrett leaned back in the leather chair. "But no matter how we get along, our firm will do whatever it takes. You've met a few people with your hearing, but we have our team of assistants, paralegals, investigators to prepare for cases. All understand that come trial time, that is the priority, and we'll have no life for a while."

He'd loved the nonstop prep before and the all-nighters during trials to make sure he knew what to say, but thinking about doing that again made Garrett's stomach roil. It wasn't like the late nights working on the booth in Taryn's backyard. That was fun.

Law used to be fun.

Used to be.

The three words reverberated through him.

Garrett was set for life with his investments, so he no longer needed the salary. Fame had done nothing but bring threats and put him under the press's microscope. He didn't need more of that. Prestige had brought clients to him, ensuring the firm thrived.

*Aren't you licensed to practice in other states besides California?*

*Yes, but I'm a partner in the firm. I need to be in L.A.*

Did he need to be in L.A., or was that what he'd told himself?

The truth was, he didn't have to be at the firm 24/7 to bring in clients. He could lighten his caseload, not retire, but limit his participation in trials and do more consulting.

And he could do that from…anywhere.

Ideas swirled.

Would this work?

"I'm the government's scapegoat. Pure and simple." Jed sat ramrod straight. "Bundling debt isn't illegal. It's not my fault they changed the rules. Investors were aware of the risk, but if they ignored it, that's on them."

Garrett focused his attention on Jed. He rarely drifted when he was with a client. "Everyone remembers what happened with junk bonds."

"Your firm is the only one that brought it up."

"Then you made the correct choice in who to represent you."

"I did, but…" Jed hung his head. "I don't want to go to jail. What are my chances?"

"No outcome is one hundred percent guaranteed, but we'll do everything in our power to prove your innocence."

Tension melted from Jed's face. "I am innocent."

The conviction in his voice was unmistakable, so was his body language.

"You are. But it'll take work to break down the case against you."

"Whatever you need to do, do it." Jed's jaw jutted forward. "I have a wife and four kids, who've I ignored for far too long to make more money. I didn't let them know what they mean to me, so I lost them. I'm ready to be a better husband and father for us to be a family again, but it'll be hard to do that from prison."

Jed's raw honesty sliced into Garrett, both professionally and personally.

"I canceled our meeting last week so that I could watch my youngest's T-ball game. That's the first event I've had in...years. My wife kept the kids away from me, and I can't blame her. But I don't want to miss another game or dance recital or band concert or nightly dinner."

Garrett wanted to help the guy so he could reunite with his family. Everyone deserved a second chance—even a third one.

As he remembered the one Taryn gave him, a lump formed in his throat. He swallowed it. "Jenn must have gone over what we do, but our first step is to get the charges dropped. Avoiding court completely is best, but if that doesn't happen, we'll put together a rock-solid case to prove your innocence. Family is everything, and you need to be with them."

Jed's gaze softened. "How long have you been married?"

"I-I'm not." The question caught Garrett off-guard.

"Oh." Jed's brows furrowed. "The way you sounded... Well, when you fall in love, here's some advice. I learned the hard way. Don't put your work first. Make sure your special person knows they matter and is your priority. No matter what. That must sound contradictory when I'm asking you to do that for me. But this is more important."

It was.

Garrett felt it deep in his bones. Except...

He clutched the chair's armrests to keep from falling over. He hadn't done that.

Not with his family—his parents and siblings.

Not with Taryn.

Money and prestige had become everything to him. Yes, he put his work first. And so did Taryn. They both had been doing the same thing. Perhaps that was why her mom and dad had been so worried about her. They hadn't wanted her to miss out on living life to the fullest because of working too much. Yet, she hadn't jumped at her dream the way he would have expected. She'd taken the time to call him—to ask him—to say she loved him.

And Garrett had the feeling if he hadn't joked about her getting on a plane and asked seriously instead, she might have done that. But why should she give up her dream when he could help the firm and be with her?

And he knew why.

His insides deflated.

Garrett was trying to prove himself. Years later, that mistake as an intern followed him, clinging to him like a leech he couldn't shake. Yet he'd made up for it in so many ways, with so many cases, but he hadn't been able to see it.

Not until today.

And he knew what he had to do. "I won't be sitting in on this case."

Jed's shoulders sagged. "I want you as lead."

"I'll be second." Garrett always gave a hundred and ten percent to his clients. But he didn't want to be that guy any longer. His heart wasn't in it. His heart belonged elsewhere—in Silver Falls with Taryn. "You've been working with Jenn. She's who you need."

"You're the best."

"I am, but I won't be the best for you right now." Garrett pictured Taryn. Warmth flowed through him. "I have other priorities."

GARRETT RETURNED TO Silver Falls like a thief in the night, parking his rental car down the street from Margot's house. That way no one—okay, Taryn—noticed it there. He paced the length of Margot's entryway with Angus and Sadie at his heels, their little paws happily following him. Air-conditioning kept the temperature cool but sweat beaded at his hairline.

Not nerves.

Anticipation.

Excitement.

Taryn was the actual thief, the one who'd stolen his heart.

The funny thing?

He didn't want it returned. Garrett would happily allow her to keep it.

Wasn't that why he was here?

The evidence was overwhelmingly clear.

Garrett wanted to be with her. Period.

The one person he trusted to help him get this right was unavailable. And that…

Sucked.

Not interrupting Callie on her honeymoon had taken strength he didn't know he possessed. But he'd done it. That left Margot to be his sounding board. She'd helped him refine each idea until he had a plan in place to ensure Taryn's and his future happiness.

"I can't wait to see her reaction."

Angus barked.

Garrett would take that as a sign of support. "Thanks, little buddy."

Margot sat on the couch. "I'm proud of you, Garrett."

"It's not like I'm giving up anything." He would travel more, but it was an easy nonstop between SEATAC and LAX. "The other partners weren't thrilled, but they didn't want to lose me either, so a compromise worked for everyone involved."

"Compromise is always key, dear. Remember that when you get married."

"I will."

"I knew the two of you belonged together."

"You didn't play matchmaker."

"Not overtly. But there may have been some subtle maneuvering behind the scenes."

Brandt would need to speak with her when he returned

from his honeymoon.

Garrett glanced at the time. Eight o'clock. That was only five minutes later than before. "Is your clock broken?"

"It works fine. Check your cell phone if you want to confirm it."

He did. "Correct."

Margot laughed. "I thought Brandt had fallen hard for Callie, but you, oh sweet barrister, take the cake."

"I don't want the cake. I want the baker."

Love. Family. Endless marionberry pie. A happily ever after.

The ringing startled him, but it wasn't his phone. Relief rushed through him.

Margot answered. "Hello."

He didn't want to eavesdrop, but what if it was Taryn?

"Garrett is right here." Margot laughed. "You have no idea. ... You and Taryn have fun tomorrow."

Not Taryn, but her mother. The plan was for Mrs. Lawson to pick up her daughter in the morning for a spa day in Summit Ridge. The day was courtesy of a gift certificate he'd provided. Dinner was on him, too. He only hoped that kept Taryn away from Main Street until nightfall.

"I know, right?" Margot winked at him. "Well, safe travels. Enjoy the spa day."

She hung up. "Mrs. Andrews is ready to do her part. Her husband is waiting for the bakery to close. Jayden will let you know the coast is clear."

"What about the others?"

"Carl and Finley are there. Brecken and Mandy will

come when Jayden calls. Keaton offered to help. Some firefighters have volunteered, which is why I'll be there."

He cocked a brow. "The hottie paramedic who likes Taryn."

"He might be there, and he's dating someone else. Rachelle rounded up several firefighters. Some of Wags and Tails's staff will be there tomorrow, too, including Anna, who wanted to represent Callie."

That sounded like something Anna would do for her best friend.

"It sounds as if half the town knows about this."

"Not half." Margot rubbed her chin. "I'd say twenty-five percent. But the most important person doesn't know. Taryn will be so surprised."

"I hope so." The dogs stared at him as if Garrett could conjure treats from thin air. He held out his hands. "Thanks for your help."

"The town and I are pulling for you."

"You mean twenty-five percent of the town."

Margot smiled slyly. "That's what I said."

He was in too good a mood to cross-examine her.

His phone rang. Jayden's name illuminated on his screen.

Garrett answered. "Hey."

"Target has left the building," Jayden whispered. "I repeat. The target has left the building."

"Why are you whispering?"

"That's what they do in the movies."

Garrett dragged his hand through his hair. "I'll be right

there."

This had the potential to go well or epically fail worse than any Pinterest fail that ever went viral. But it was the thought that counted, and he hoped Taryn agreed.

He disconnected from the call. "Wish me luck."

"You don't need luck." Margot had her purse strap on her shoulder and car keys in hand. "You're in love. That's all you need."

The knot of unease loosened in his gut. "Let's go make Taryn's dream come true."

# Chapter Twenty-Two

M ONDAY MORNING, TARYN woke before her alarm clock rang, not bothering to peer out the window. All she would see was darkness, but it matched her mood. Taryn missed Garrett. He'd texted her yesterday, but she'd spent the day with her mom, so she hadn't been able to speak to him. He hadn't answered when she called him last night. Garrett must have been working on a Sunday.

He needed to cut his hours.

*You're one to talk.*

Truth. She laughed. But she was planning a vacation in Los Angeles.

She'd impressed her dad with her business plan and ideas. He admitted he'd been trying to make her quit this past year because he and her mother worried she was becoming a workaholic. She had been, but she promised to work on balancing her life better, and he said he would communicate with her better.

Progress.

If only she could make the same with Garrett.

But nothing—not even the lovely spa day with her mom yesterday—stopped her from missing him. She tried to lose herself in baking, but wherever she turned in the kitchen, memories of him surfaced.

Forcing herself out of bed, she French-braided her hair and put on her uniform. That way, she could get right to work, preparing for the morning rush, since she would be the first one at the bakery. She put the lanyard with her keys around her neck. The only things missing?

Her hairnet and cap.

Those were in the office.

Her appetite had been nonexistent, so she didn't make a cup of coffee. She locked her front door and headed toward First Avenue.

No one was out at this hour. Occasionally, a car passed by, but usually, she was the only one out. The stillness might freak some out, but not Taryn. She enjoyed walking through the town before it woke to start the day.

The lights on the storefronts of First Avenue were dark, but the streetlamps illuminated the sidewalk. Taryn un-locked the bakery's front door, opened the door with the comforting ding, and locked the door again from the inside, hearing another chime.

She flipped on the lights.

*Time to do this.*

Taryn turned.

Gasped.

Fresh paint covered the walls. Someone had replaced all the tables and chairs. The fixtures, too. Only…

"It looks like my vision board."

Well, minus the signs, which she had planned to make herself.

This had to be a dream.

She squeezed her eyes shut and opened them.

Still there.

She pinched herself. "Ouch."

Feeling pain meant she wasn't asleep, and this was real.

A thrill shot through her.

But how? Who?

She floated to the new front counter and ran her fingertips along the surface. Everything was perfect, exactly as she imagined when she pored over magazines and catalogs.

Footsteps sounded in the kitchen.

Taryn straightened. "Jayden."

Garrett came out. He wore a Lawson's Bakery apron and a white cap over his white shirt and jeans. "Welcome to Lawson's Bakery."

She glanced around as if someone would jump out and explain what was going on, but no one appeared. "I don't understand."

He rocked back on his heels. "The night before Callie and Brandt's wedding, I saw your plans for the remodel. I wanted to do this for you."

"You?"

Garrett nodded. "This is your dream, and I want it to come true."

"Thank you." Tears blurred her vision. She blinked. It didn't help. "I wish—"

"The other part of your dream would come true, too."

Once again, he read her so well. She nodded.

"It can."

She startled. "Say what?"

"Both of your dreams are coming true, Taryn." He wiped his hand on the front of the apron. "You're right. I can work anywhere, but you can't take this place with you. Lawson's Bakery is part of your family. It's your legacy. And I want to help you make it a success."

She sniffled. "I love you."

He went around the counter to stand next to her. "I love you."

Her heart skipped a beat. "I can't believe this is happening."

"Believe. And I…"

"What?"

"I want to move to Silver Falls. But even though I have responsibilities as a partner in the firm, and I'm a major rainmaker, I don't have to take on cases as the lead attorney. I can consult."

"You love your work. Why would you do that?"

"Because I can't imagine my life without you in it." He took a breath. "I love you, and we will make this work. You can come to L.A. with me sometimes. But Silver Falls will be our home base. I want to help you make Lawson's into the bakery of your dreams. That's why I had to be here, at this ridiculous hour, to see your face when you arrived. Whatever it takes. Though my baking skills leave a lot to be desired, I'm happy to learn because I believe in you. And in us."

Her heart pounded. Taryn was in shock, feeling as if she were still dreaming, but she wanted to believe it was real— true.

Contentment flowed through her. "We can do it together. And Jayden's a manager now, and we're hiring more staff, so that will give me more free time to go to Los Angeles with you. I miss you when we're apart."

"I missed you so much." He cupped her face. "I love

you, Taryn. I love how caring you are, how generous and loyal and kind, how organized you are, and how you bake incredible desserts. I love your creativity and your dimples. I love your kisses and every single thing about you."

Tears of happiness welled in her eyes. This had to be a dream, right? "I love you."

He rested his forehead against her. "We can go slow, whatever it takes. Just tell me you're in it for the long term."

"I am." She placed her hand over his heart and felt the beat against her palm. "We shared a slice of summer, but I'm in this forever."

"Okay, since you said forever." He dropped onto one knee, removed the ring box from his pocket, and opened it.

Taryn gasped. She covered her mouth with her hands.

"I can't imagine my life without you in it." Garrett held out the ring. "Will you marry me?"

Taryn dropped to her knees. "Yes, of course, I'll marry you."

He put the ring on her finger. A perfect fit. "I love you."

The diamond shot prisms around the bakery. She sighed.

"Thanks for making my dreams come true and loving me." She raised her chin and kissed him on the lips. "I love you so much."

## The End

Want more? Check out Callie and Brandt's story in *The Christmas Window*!

Join Tule Publishing's newsletter for more great reads and weekly deals!

If you enjoyed *A Slice of Summer*,
you'll love the other book in the…

## Silver Falls series

Book 1: *The Christmas Window*

Book 2: *A Slice of Summer*

*Available now at your favorite online retailer!*

# More books by Melissa McClone

## Ever After series

A pair of best friends, a prince looking for a bride, and an unexpected royal match… Could they all possibly live happily ever after?

Book 1: *The Honeymoon Prize*

Book 2: *The Cinderella Princess*

Book 3: *Christmas at the Castle*

## Bar V5 Ranch series

The Bar V5 Ranch of Marietta, Montana: where love is found in the most unexpected places.

Book 1: *Home for Christmas*

Book 2: *Mistletoe Magic*

Book 3: *Kiss Me, Cowboy*

Book 4: *Mistletoe Wedding*

Book 5: *A Christmas Homecoming*

*Available now at your favorite online retailer!*

# About the Author

With a degree in mechanical engineering from Stanford University, Melissa McClone worked for a major airline where she traveled the globe and met her husband. But analyzing jet engine performance couldn't compete with her love of writing happily ever afters. She's now a USA Today Bestselling author and has also been nominated for Romance Writers of America's RITA® award. Melissa lives in the Pacific Northwest with her husband, three children, a spoiled Norwegian Elkhound, and cats who think they rule the house. They do!

Thank you for reading

# A Slice of Summer

If you enjoyed this book, you can find more from all our great authors at TulePublishing.com, or from your favorite online retailer.

TULE
PUBLISHING